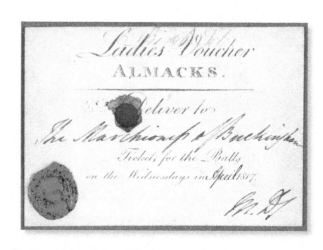

*A voucher for Almacks.*

# Anarchy at Almacks

## A STORY OF LOVE AT FIRST SIGHT

### Nola Saint James

THE EDANMORE CHRONICLES
BOOK ONE

Nemeton Press | New York City

Cover and book design: Kelly Duke McKinley, theshopkeys.com
Illustrations by Madeline McKinley

ISBN: 978-0-9978428-8-3

*For E of Mattituck, with boundless gratitude…*

*For Neil, my hero, who has always insisted that
I am a writer…*

*For Jim Willy, creative partner and task master
extraordinaire. Without you…*

*For Anita Gilodo, counselor and friend, who
saved my life and ultimately made this book possible…*

*My love and thanks to all of you.*

"When a man is tired of London,
he is tired of life; for there is in London
all that life can afford."

— SAMUEL JOHNSON

## INTRODUCTION

Welcome to the Regency World of Nola Saint James!

Once upon a time, there was a family living on a small island in the Celtic Sea. Then they journeyed to London for the Season ...

# CONTENTS

*"All the world's a stage ... "*
—WILLIAM SHAKESPEARE

# WHO'S WHO IN
## *Anarchy at Almacks*

## Our Heroine
**Rowan Bryn Higbee,** due to her unusual upbringing, is adept
in the use of many different weapons. At 22 years old, she has
the reddest hair of all three sisters, and expressive dark-blue
eyes. Of medium height, she is extremely athletic and is an
outstanding equestrienne.

## Rowan's Parents
**James Marius Ian Higbee, 9th Baron Edanmore,** is
70 years old, heavyset (but not fat), just under 6 feet tall,
robust. His bright blue eyes accentuate his bushy sideburns
and somewhat faded ginger hair. He is madly in love with
his wife.

**Rose Sharon Byrne Higbee,** the present Baroness Edanmore,
53 years old, red-haired and blue-eyed, spirited in word and
deed, dedicated to marrying off all her unmarried children and
stepchildren.

## Rowan's Sisters
**Willow Blair Higbee,** 20 years old, has straight, orange-gold
hair, large hazel eyes and a tall, thin, graceful body. She has
a deep knowledge of healing with herbs and music as well
as traditional medicine. She loves nature and animals. A fey
quality enhances her beauty.

**Ivy Brianna Higbee,** 18 years old, has carrot-red curly hair and green eyes. She is diminutive with lots of curves— a true pocket Venus. Ivy is also extremely intuitive and loves solving all types of puzzles.

## Four of Rowan's Eight Stepbrothers

**Blake Horatio Higbee,** 44 years old, has red hair and hazel eyes. He is married to the daughter of the Duke of Surrey, Lady Mary Anne Clark. They have five children. Blake works for the Home Office in an undefined capacity.

**Broderick Sean Higbee-James,** 42 years old, is just under six feet tall. He has golden red hair and blue eyes. Broderick is a financial genius and the investment counselor for the family. His father-in-law, Evan James, had no sons. A stipulation in the marriage contract was that Broderick take the James name.

**Brian Gerald Higbee,** 40 years old, has chestnut blond hair, hazel eyes and is an accomplished architect. He is married to Marie-Louise Aubery, the daughter of the very wealthy Comte de Lorainne. She is a noted designer of interiors.

**Benedict Connor Higbee,** 34 years old, is unwilling to relinquish his bachelor status. He has gold-streaked, dark auburn hair, flashing green eyes and the muscular build of a horseman. In partnership with his father, he runs Edanmore Stud, a premier horse breeding and training facility in Newmarket.

## Our Hero
**Max, Lord Maximillian Francis Browning, Viscount Darby, heir to the 7th Earl of Bainbridge,** is 29 years old. He has worked for the Admiralty as a spy for the past seven years. Max is tall, with shiny black hair worn clubbed back, dark coffee-brown eyes and a muscular physique. An apex Corinthian with a slightly rakish reputation, Max carries himself like a man used to getting himself out of tricky situations.

## Max's Best Friend
**Grey, Lord Richard Grey Birmingham, 9th Earl of Wellesly Glen,** is almost 30 years old and unmarried. Grey has a wiry frame, chestnut blond hair worn unfashionably short, hazel eyes and a cleft in his chin. Grey has a great many match-making aunts.

## The Troublemakers
**Gerard Fontaine,** 21 years old, is the younger son of **Lord John William Fontaine and Lady Sybil Gertrude Fontaine, Viscount and Viscountess Edgeby.** Gerard has light brown hair, dark brown eyes, is socially awkward and easily led, especially by a pretty woman.

**Lady Flavia St John,** 22 years old, is the elder of twins born to **Lord Percival and Lady Eugenia St John, Viscount and Viscountess Somersby.** She has dark brown, short curly hair, a heart-shaped face, a razor-sharp nose and bright hazel eyes. She also has most of the brains in her family.

**Lord Frederick St John, Baron Hilton,** 22 years old, is Flavia's younger twin. He has curly brown hair and brown eyes. He does whatever his twin tells him to do and has no ideas of his own.

*"Aristocratic noses were bloodied
and broken ... "*

# PROLOGUE

**London, the beginning of the Season**
*The Ton Reporter,* **Thursday, April 5, 1804**

*If last night's riot at Almacks is any indication, the Season of 1804 is going to prove to be of unprecedented interest. More blood was spilled on the hallowed floors of London's most exclusive meeting place for single ladies and gentlemen than one might find on the ground trod by two champion bare-knuckle boxers.*

*Aristocratic noses were bloodied and broken as the ton's Pinks and Corinthians fought their way across the dance floor toward the evening's main attraction — three lovely, flame-haired sisters from the idyllic isle of Edanmore. The breathtaking Higbee sisters — the Misses Rowan, 22, Willow, 20 and Ivy, 18 — seemed unperturbed by the pandemonium that resulted from their mere entrance into Almacks hallowed halls. Anyone seeing them together might have cautioned their parents to bring them out one at time. Any one of them would be the Diamond of her season! But put them all together? A riot at Almacks may only be the first of such events during this season. Indeed, Parliament may well have to pass a law prohibiting the three young ladies from appearing together in public, in order to keep the peace!*

*As the melee increased in volume, combativeness, the crunching of bones and the flowing of blood, other young ladies, fresh from the country, fainted dead away. Virile young men fighting to stake their claim on the ton's newest arrivals, was unique in the history of that hallowed hall.*

—S. J. ROBERTS, SOCIETY REPORTER

*Almacks — Wednesday, April 4, 1804.*

# CHAPTER ONE
## *Mayhem at Almacks!*

*It is the duty of the eldest sister to set an example for the sisters who come after her. She should not attempt to be perfect or to mimic perfection. She should just try to do her best. She should always be honest with her sisters about her missteps. By her honesty, they will learn that life is not about our triumphs, but about how we manage our failures. By her good example, when her sisters make their own mistakes, they will know that it is possible to pick oneself up and move on.*

— *Lady X's Admonitions to Young Women (Third Edition, 1802)*

**Almacks Assembly Rooms**
**Wednesday, April 4, 1804 – The night before**

"Great God in Heaven! Who?" Lord Maximillian Francis Browning, Max to his friends, couldn't say another word. He grabbed the shoulders of his boon companion, Lord Richard

Grey Birmingham, and forcefully spun him around to face the entranceway to Almacks ballroom. It was the first Wednesday of the Season, and the room was buzzing in the anticipation of a new crop of young ladies making their come outs.

Both men gazed in wonder at a trio of stunning, red-haired young ladies who had just entered Almacks' hallowed halls. They were chaperoned by a distinguished older couple, obviously their parents.

"Good Lord!" cried Grey. "I heard about the Higbee sisters from my mother, but I never imagined that they looked like that."

"The one with the darkest red hair?"

"That's Miss Rowan Higbee, the eldest sister," said a woman's voice behind him.

Max turned and looked into the kind, blue eyes of his mother's dearest friend, Lady Saxby.

"I met their mother one summer when I spent some time on Edanmore Island. All the young women are lovely."

At just that moment, the sister with the darkest red hair, Miss Rowan, caught Max's dark brown eyes. Her shining sapphire-blue eyes seemed to pierce his soul. Max felt as though he had stopped breathing. From somewhere deep within, he heard a voice shout, "It is she!"

Then, "Mine!"

Without realizing it, Max began to move towards the woman he now thought of as his Rowan. The voice prodded him, "Go. Go to her. This is really and truly love!"

"This is it," thought Max as he began to move toward his soon-to-be wife. He was somewhat taller than most of the men in the ballroom and could keep Rowan in sight as he moved across the room. Grey, an inch shorter, with the muscular build of a man who regularly worked the land, walked slightly ahead of him. The roiling mass of humanity parted before them. As they made their way toward the entrance, Lady Sefton, one of the patronesses of Almacks, came forward to greet the family, all smiles.

"Have you ever?" asked Max.

"Never!" said Grey.

Had Max been less entranced, he would have realized he was not the only man making his way in the direction of the three young women. It was as if they were magnets to whom the gentlemen in the room were irresistibly attracted.

As the mass of men moved forward, they began jostling one another. Because Almacks did not serve spirits, some of the men had imbibed heavily before appearing at the assembly hall. In their alcohol-fueled haze, they began to object to being hindered from reaching the three young beauties.

Unexpected collisions began to occur. Voices were raised. More deliberate shoving commenced. Fists began to fly. A few noses were broken. Blood began to flow. Before anyone could stop it, a full-scale riot had broken out. Some young ladies fainted. Others shrieked in alarm. A few women were secretly thrilled!

The impact of these lovely ladies was felt not only by the young bucks! The venerable Duke of B — well into his eighth decade, was seen slowly shuffling to their side. Thankfully, because of his exalted status in the ton, everyone gave him a wide berth. Several of the dowagers present surrounded him to assure that he was not jostled.

Lady Sefton and several other patronesses surrounded the family and whisked them away to a private room where they could wait for their carriage.

## *The Ton Reporter,* The Fashion Page
## Thursday, April 5, 1804

*The riot at Almacks last night (see S. J. Roberts news report) might not have occurred had not the family of the Baron Edanmore been accepted as a client of the renowned modiste, Madame Celeste Laval. The three flame-haired sisters were dressed in ensembles crafted by this unparalleled gift to London's world of fashion.*

*Miss Rowan Higbee was dressed in a creation — one cannot call it simply a gown — of royal-blue silk with an overlay of tissue-thin white lace embellished with tiny diamonds. To say she was breathtaking would be a gross understatement. Tiny diamond pins could be seen shyly peeking out of her curls, which were arranged in a cluster all over her head. Around her neck, she wore a perfectly spherical solitary pearl as big as a quail's egg, suspended on a silver chain so delicate that it seemed as though the pearl hovered in thin air above her décolletage. Would it fall? The suspense was heart-stopping!*

*Smaller pearls, equally perfect, were suspended from the lady's delicate ear lobes. They moved with her every step, seeming to be in communion with her very breath. Taken all together, Miss Higbee seemed like nothing less than the essence of twilight that had drifted into the room bringing the moon and stars with her. What is more, she seemed completely unconscious of the fact that she put the angels to shame.*

Miss Willow, who is the tallest of the three sisters, has the lightest red hair, an arresting pale orange gold that is straight and extremely silky. She wore it pulled back and woven into an elaborate knot high on the back of her head.

Her gown was the compelling green of an ancient-growth forest, but with a sheen that made it seem as though the gown was constantly changing colors. The blue of a clear morning sky, the darker blue/grey of early evening and a hint of red at sundown constantly swirled around her. The dress featured a flowing train that hung from Miss Willow's shoulders.

To complement her ensemble, she wore a delicate gold net collar that hugged her neck and then descended to just above the top of her bodice. It was studded with emeralds, sapphires and rubies. In her ears, she wore emerald stud earrings. Rather than making her seem like a fabulously wealthy heiress — which she may or may not be, the combination of gown and jewels seemed to enhance an innate "fey" quality that seems to be a natural and unconscious part of her being.

Miss Ivy, the youngest of the three sisters at just 18, is Venus in miniature. She is all carrot-red curls, luminous green eyes, skin the color of wave foam and generous curves perfectly suited to her diminutive proportions. The lady exudes an air of kindness, and her eyes seem to notice everything around her. When she became aware of the fracas, her immediate and generous impulse was to rush to the aid of the fallen men. She was gently restrained by her mother, who needed only to place her hand gently on her daughter's shoulder to prevent the girl's movement.

This lovely young woman was dressed in white, which is de rigueur for the youngest of young ladies making their come out. To say it was a "white dress" would be to say that a glorious sunrise is just the sun coming up.

Madame Laval's true genius is that her fashions, in their restraint, permit the personality of the wearer to shine through. It wouldn't surprise this writer at all if there is not some sorcery involved. In the case of Miss Ivy, Madame's creation highlighted the young lady's natural sweetness and modesty, while gently suggesting that she is so much more. Miss Ivy wore a simple, white-silk sheath that tastefully displayed her assets to best advantage. The scalloped neckline was higher than usual but in covering up it also emphasized Miss Ivy's charms. The short, slightly puffed sleeves were slashed and inset with thin strips of gold velvet. The pleats at the back of her dress were also lined with the same material.

Her lovely carrot-red curls were studded with small emerald pins. Around her neck, she wore a simple circlet of fire opals with matching stones in her ears. To call that necklace simple is a misnomer. It was as though all the good spirits residing on the idyllic island of Edanmore were surrounding her with their love and joy. In all, Miss Ivy was the ideal presentation of all that a young lady making her debut should be.

Our sources tell us that a debut ball for the three sisters is being planned for some time later this season. It will take place at Edanmore House, which has recently been renovated and decorated by the baron's fourth son, noted architect, Mr. Brian Higbee, assisted by his talented wife, the daughter of the Comte de Lorainne. It is said that the baron spared no expense in the decoration and furnishing of the house. In addition, the *installation of the newest conveniences reportedly includes the piping of heated water to bathing rooms on every floor.*

*A word to the young men of the ton planning to attend Almacks next Wednesday: "Keep a sober head!" The impact of the Flame Sisters may, in time, lessen as we mere mortals are exposed to their allure. In the meantime, maintaining one's faculties is strongly advised.*

*Illustrations of the ensembles created by Madame Laval for the Flame Sisters for their first appearance at Almacks can be found below this article. We thank Madame for supplying these with the permission of Baron Edanmore.*

*What spectacle will the Flame Sisters ignite in the weeks ahead?*

*No one knew it then, but what was later to be remembered as "The Season of the Flame Sisters" had just begun.*

*"Never, in all their fantasies about their presentation at Almacks, had the young women considered that they might create a riot!"*

# CHAPTER TWO
## *When Sisters Gather.*

*Should you be lucky enough to have even one sister,*
*keep her close. And more than one? You are truly blessed. As*
*you shared your mother's womb, so, too, can you share the*
*dearest secrets of your heart with your sisters. They will guard*
*them more surely than even your most trusted friend. And if a*
*sister should betray your trust, you must castigate her in the*
*strongest terms, even to a stinging slap on the wrist! Thus,*
*shall she learn she must never break faith with you again!*

*— Lady X's Admonitions to Young Women (Third Edition, 1802)*

Later that night, after the riot at Almacks, Rowan, Willow
and Ivy sat around a beautiful marble inlaid table in their
sitting room at Edanmore House. They were dressed in soft
cashmere robes — pale blue for Rowan, soft golden bronze
for Willow and white for Ivy — and were sharing a pot of hot

chocolate and scones with raspberry jam and clotted cream.

It had been an eventful evening. Never, in all their fantasies about their presentation at Almacks, had the young women considered that they might create a riot! They had never created a riot on Edanmore Island. But then, on Edanmore, they had never been outfitted by London's most sought-after modiste, Madame Celeste Laval!

"Madame was there!" Ivy said. "She saw it all! Do you think she was pleased?"

"I think she must have been in alt," replied Willow, "or at least as much in alt as she ever is. I believe that she would think of it as her due! A testament to her genius!"

"She is a genius," said Rowan. "All we did was enter and stand there. Did you see the look on the men's faces? It was funny, in a strange sort of way. They looked like they'd been hit over the head with a mallet. I've never seen men look like that!"

"They looked like they'd been put under a sorceress's spell," said Ivy. She was still very much in thrall of novels that spoke of witch's spells and enchantments. "They were fighting one another to get to us! There was blood!"

"It was like seeing a strange type of love potion at work," said Willow.

"Do you think it will be like that all Season?" asked Ivy. "How are we going to meet our own true loves if the men are so dumbstruck that they can't see us? Us as the women we are?"

"I'm sure that Madame has planned for that," said Rowan.

"How did mama and papa feel about it, do you think?" asked Willow.

"I think that papa was secretly delighted!" said Rowan.

"You know how much he loves to play tricks on people. This whole spectacle, renovating this palace, and the new carriages and the horses and the clothes! It's a huge lark to him. I think he's in his element."

"This all seems to be making mama happy as well," said Ivy. "I know that they both love living on Edanmore, but they haven't left it in forever except for short excursions within Ireland and Scotland! I'm glad we decided to make our come outs together. It's going to be so much fun to share the Season! Mama told me that all our brothers will be coming to see us with their wives and children."

"Benedict is coming from Newmarket," Rowan told them. Benedict was their father's sixth son and an expert on everything with four legs, especially horses. With his father as a silent partner, he owned and operated Edanmore Stud, a horse-breeding and training facility in Newmarket. Of all the eight Higbee sons, he was the only one left unmarried.

"Mama told me that Benedict is going to spend a great deal of time here, and will help escort us during the Season," continued Rowan.

"Mama told me," said Ivy with a tone of self-importance, "that he's bringing us mounts!"

"Ooooh," sighed her other two sisters. All three of them loved horses and were bruising riders. On Edanmore, they rode astride, but had learned to ride sidesaddle in preparation for their trip to London.

"I'm so excited!" said Willow. "Benedict is sure to bring us the very best horses he can find. Now that you've told us that, Ivy, I can hardly wait!"

"With all that pushing and shoving at Almacks," said

Ivy, "were any of you able to pick out a gentleman you found compelling?" asked Ivy. In the novels she read, strangers seeing one another across a crowded room was a frequent theme.

"There were so many of them!" replied Willow. "And the scene became a brawl so quickly! There was hardly any time at all to get a good look at individual gentlemen."

Willow and Ivy turned to Rowan and then at one another. Rowan was blushing!

"You saw someone!" crowed Ivy. "You saw him across the crowded room!" She was exultant in her joy.

"No, no, not really," replied Rowan, blushing more furiously.

"Yes, really!" cried Ivy. "You did! Don't deny it! You know I love puzzles and that I'll figure it out anyway. Tell us all!

Rowan took a deep breath.

"It was just a moment, really," she said. "Just a flash of an instant. Hardly worth speaking of at all."

"I think you really must tell us!" said Willow. "You're blushing! Rowan Bryn Higbee! You never blush! You didn't even blush when we saw the Corwin brothers in the altogether at the pond! And you looked at them for a whole two minutes!"

"It was one minute!" responded Rowan testily. "And I barely peeked at them!"

"Tell all!" demanded Ivy.

Rowan smiled. She could never fool her sisters. She began her story.

"He was standing directly across the room under one of the chandeliers. He was bathed in light, almost as though there was a glow all around him. He was tall, and he held himself like a man used to getting himself out of tricky situations."

"What does that mean?" asked Ivy. "And how could you possibly tell that from all the way across a ballroom?"

"There was something about him," responded Rowan. "A sense that he was completely in charge of his world and everything in it. I can't explain it, but it was almost as though there was a band of angels surrounding him and they were blowing trumpets!"

"Ooooh," sighed Ivy. "That's so romantic!"

"What did he look like?" asked Willow.

"He had black hair. It was clubbed back. He was dressed impeccably. It looked almost as though his garments were painted onto his body."

Ivy giggled. "I can't believe that you just said that!" she exclaimed. "Tell us more!"

Rowan continued.

"He was wearing a large dark jewel in his cravat. It was too far away to be sure, but I think it was a sapphire in an intricate gold setting. It looked like a very old piece. I couldn't tell the exact color of his eyes, but they were very dark and mysterious. He looked brooding."

"I'm in love!" interrupted Ivy. "If you don't want him, I'll take him."

Rowan and Willow laughed.

"Tell us more," urged Willow.

"When I was looking at him," said Rowan, "it was as though I could see into his soul! You know that gramma says all the women in our family have the Sight. I never believed it before, but I do now. For a moment, it was as though I could see the future. He and I and a lot of children. We were together in some place I didn't recognize, and we were laughing!"

"He's your own true love!" shouted Ivy.

"I think she may be right," said Willow, somewhat more quietly.

"I think so, too," confessed Rowan. "I think he may be the one, but I have no idea who he is! And what if I actually meet him and he's terrible? What if he doesn't have a brain in his head?"

"It sounds like he's gorgeous!" said Ivy. "If he isn't so smart, maybe you could marry him and tell him that you like men who don't say very much! Or don't let him talk at all! Tell him just to nod and make gestures and that you'll love him forever!"

The three sisters laughed so hard that tears ran down their cheeks.

There was a knock on the door, and their mother, Rose, walked in. She smiled at them.

"Why so merry, my girls?" she asked. She loved to see her daughters happy. They were her pride and joy.

"Rowan may have seen her fated husband!" announced Ivy.

"Really, Rowan?" said their mother, turning to her eldest daughter. "It's unlike you to make such quick judgements."

"Come sit down, mother," said Rowan leading her mother to one of the well-padded chairs. "I'll tell you all about it."

The girls sat down on the beautiful Persian carpet in front of their mother and took turns telling Rowan's story. When they had finished, their mother said, "That's quite a tale."

"But what if he really is my fated husband and I never actually meet him? London is so big and there are so many people in it! Or what if he meets someone else and marries her? Or what if he didn't really see me? What if I'm not his fated wife?" Rowan asked her mother.

"My dearest, sweetest girl," Rowan's mother said, "If he is truly your fated husband, all will work out as it should. You need do nothing except go on with your life and continue being your own wonderful self. And if he's not the one, the right man will appear. The Season is just beginning. You will be meeting many men. You need only relax and enjoy yourself. And that is true for all of you.

"And now it's time for bed, girls. There's much to do tomorrow. We can expect a great many callers, and you all need to be well rested. Since we returned from Almacks a few hours ago, your father has received three letters from gentlemen wishing to meet with him to discuss courting you! He even received a proposal of marriage — for any one of you willing to entertain the gentleman's suit! This is unprecedented. And ridiculous!

"You mustn't worry. We both want all of you to marry for love. We won't entertain any requests from gentlemen without consulting you first. We want you to enjoy yourselves. And if you don't find matches this year, we can return in the fall or even next spring for as long as you wish to do so. There is no hurry and no pressure. And if you decide that you don't want to marry, you will have enough money to determine how and where you would like to live. But I do so hope that each of you will find your happily ever after."

They rose to wish their mother good night. Rose hugged Rowan and kissed her on her cheek. "Sleep well my precious one," she said. She hugged Willow and kissed her on her forehead, "Sweet dreams, my treasure," she whispered. She hugged Ivy and kissed her on the tip of her nose. "May the angels sing you to sleep, my young one," she said, as if in prayer. She had almost lost Ivy at birth, and was always the most anxious about her youngest daughter.

The sisters circled their mother and hugged her and hugged one another, their evening ritual. Then they all went off to bed.

Rowan loved her bedroom in their London house. A year before the family's trip to London for the Season, Rowan's father had hired his fourth son, Brian, an up-and-coming architect to completely renovate Edanmore House. Brian's wife, Marie-Louise, who was a talented designer of interiors, had been hired to decorate the ramshackle building and make it a home. The house's proximity to St James's Palace, as well as its enormous size, had offered unique challenges to the talented couple. Everyone in the family agreed that the renovation was a great success.

Marie-Louise had written to each of Brian's sisters and had asked them about their favorite colors, their taste in decoration and even how they spent their time on Edanmore. She was aware that the sisters had never had their own rooms in Hightower Castle on Edanmore Island. The girls had shared a large dormitory room, ostensibly because it was the warmest room in the house. The truth had a much more interesting explanation.

Several years after their father's third son had been born, his first wife, Mary Anne, had complained that the three boys were constantly fighting. After some discussion, the baron and his wife came up with a cunning plan. They gave the warmest bedroom with the biggest bed to their eldest son. The other two had their own rooms, which were considerably colder.

It took the boys a couple of weeks to figure out that all three of them could share a bed in the warm room at night. In the early morning, the younger boys would sneak back to their own beds. It was, they believed, a secret of which their parents were unaware. This arrangement could only work if all the boys were getting along together. Otherwise, the eldest son could send his brothers back to their own cold rooms.

From that time on, harmony reigned at Hightower Castle. When all the boys left home, their mother having died, the baron and his new wife, Rose, decided to create a shared dormitory in the "warm room" for their growing family of girls. Each girl had her own bed and personal space, but they all had the knowledge that their sisters were nearby. If any of them had a bad dream, a sister was always nearby to offer comfort.

Their move to Edanmore House in London signaled a new change in sisters' relationship. Each young woman would now have her own room for the first time. Marie-Louise had set about creating a personal sanctuary for each of them.

The sisters had their own wing in Edanmore House. All the rooms looked out onto the park at the back of the house. Each bedroom door was painted in the favorite color of each sister. The door to Rowan's room was red.

Rowan looked around her bedroom. To call the room a bedroom was a misnomer. It was actually a suite with a parlor and its own bathing room. It was a sanctuary beyond Rowan's wildest dreams.

The room was light and airy. The walls were covered with a cream-colored paper-hanging decorated with small clusters of rowan berries and rowan leaves on delicate branches. The long satin drapes around the window were green with thin cream stripes. The curtains around her bed were light green velvet tied back with cream-colored ribbons. The effect was soothing and interesting. As she was admiring her room, Hélène, Rowan's maid, knocked lightly on the door and entered.

"All the servants below stairs are abuzz, Mademoiselle," she said. "They said that there was a riot at Almacks when you and your sisters arrived! Madame Laval will be so pleased!" Rowan laughed. "She will be, indeed!" she replied as Hélène began to help her out of her robe and into a soft white cotton night rail trimmed in delicate lace. Madame had had the letter R embroidered in bright pink silk on the left side of the gown near Rowan's heart. Rowan and her sisters had helped one another out of their gowns earlier.

"I admit to being a little sorry for the other young ladies whose first evening at Almacks was eclipsed by our arrival," Rowan continued.

"Pah!" responded her maid. "Those little cats would be the first to shred you and your sisters to pieces if you had not been so splendidly attired! Don't waste your sympathies on them! The ones who will become your friends will be the young ladies who call tomorrow and laugh with you about the sight of all the bewitched young men trying to get to the three of you."

"I hope you're right," said Rowan. "It would be wonderful to have some friends of our age in town."

During this conversation, Rowan was removing the pins from her hair. She placed them carefully in a small ebony box that had been a gift from her father on her 16th birthday, when she had begun to put up her hair.

Released from the pins, her gleaming bright red hair fell in heavy waves past her shoulder blades. Rowan began to brush her hair. This simple evening ritual helped to give her a sense of normalcy.

Rowan knew that Hélène would perform this task for her, but she insisted on doing this for herself. Before she and sisters had come to London, they had dressed themselves and helped one another put up their hair. Life on Edanmore was much more casual and easygoing. Having a personal servant to see to such intimate tasks was a change that would take some time to get used to. Madame had explained that ladies of the ton needed such attentions to make sure that they were perfectly turned out, and that their clothes were properly taken care of. Rowan understood that such help was important when one was leaving the house, but why would she need such assistance before going to bed?

An errant thought came into her head. Did going to bed with one's husband require being specially turned out? Ladies' maids were almost always single. How would they know what to do to make a woman desirable to her husband? Was there a book that she could read so that she would know what her future husband might wish of her? To whom could she pose such a delicate question?

*"The dream, which had haunted her for a number of years, sprang into being."*

# CHAPTER THREE
## Rowan's Dream.

*Young women would be wise to weigh every word young men say, especially as those words refer to the young lady's form, face and character. If such words are followed by an invitation to stroll in the woods, unchaperoned, beware! If his words are sincere, he will not use them to lure a young woman into an indiscretion.*

— *Lady X's Admonitions to Young Women (Third Edition, 1802)*

The clean, fresh smell of the linen bedclothes and the weight of the down blanket always made Rowan feel as if she was crawling into a cocoon. She huddled down into the mattress, pulled the blanket around her and quickly fell asleep.

The question about what might be necessary to ready oneself for one's husband followed Rowan into sleep and pushed her dreaming mind into troubling thoughts. The dream, which had haunted her for a number of years, sprang into being. It held the memory of her darkest moments. As much as she wished that the dream would disappear and never come back, it seemed to occur whenever she found herself in a new situation.

The dream always began the same way. Rowan was on Edanmore, that lovely Eden which had nurtured her and given her so many wonderful things. It was summer, and Rowan had just turned 16. She had climbed the highest hill behind the castle and was looking out across the vast expanse of water that surrounded her home. What delights lay beyond that sea, she wondered. Was her true love waiting for her, wondering when she would walk into his life and fulfill all the dreams of his aching heart?

There was so much more to the world than her beloved island of Edanmore! Odd feelings of rebellion — she knew not exactly against what — had recently taken over both her waking and sleeping mind. Things that she had always taken for granted and enjoyed — her family, her home, the routine of the schoolroom — had begun to feel like "not enough." She yearned for something she could not describe. She had begun to dream of love, of meeting a wonderful man who, seeing her for the first time, would fall to his knees, proclaim his undying devotion to her, and carry her away to a life filled with adventure and mystery. She had read Romeo and Juliette that past winter, and had cried copious tears for the young lovers so cruelly denied a life together. She kept the book under her pillow and read the most heart-rending passages over and over again.

In her dream, Rowan spied a young man covering the rolling hills with a compelling, confident stride. Even from far away, she knew that this was a stranger. The only young man of her acquaintance who walked with such a sense of ownership of the land and all he surveyed, was her eldest brother, Brendon, her father's heir. It couldn't be Brendon, because he was presently in London taking care of some business for their father. Besides, this young man had blond hair. Brendon had brown hair with streaks of red.

Rowan watched him, wondering where he was going. He looked like a man on a mission. She would like to know what that mission was, but of course she couldn't just run up to him and ask. He was a stranger, and they hadn't been introduced. This was one of the few rules of polite behavior — that's what her mother called them — that their mother had drummed into them. The scene faded and Rowan awoke.

Rowan sat bolt upright. She remembered the Summer Festival nine years ago that her parents had sponsored. Everyone on the island gathered at the castle early in the day to claim their spots for the picnic lunch. Long tables of simple foods were set up, and guests would select their preferences and then sit and talk with friends. Glasses of ale and lemonade were available for all. One special table was laden with all types of biscuits and sliced cakes.

After lunch and a suitable period of rest for the older folks, there were games of all sorts for young and old alike. One of the favorites was an archery contest: one for young men and one for young women. A silver trophy was given to each of the winners. At the age of 13, Rowan had been retired from competition because she had won the girls' event three years in a row. She longed to compete against the men.

Rowan had brought her request to her parents as they were finishing breakfast one day a few weeks before the event the year she had turned thirteen. She had explained, in her most mature language, that while she didn't think she could really win against the oldest boys, she knew that she could easily outshoot at least some of the younger contestants. She would not disgrace the barony by coming in last. Would they permit her to shoot against the boys in the archery contest? She had waited anxiously for her parents' response. She had been sure that they would agree with her assessment of the situation.

Rowan remembered the unspoken conversation between her parents, because she had never been aware of their communicating like that before. Her father had looked at her mother, his head tilted slightly to one side, a soft smile on his face. Rowan believed that he was on her side. Her mother had gazed into her husband's eyes, looking a little sad. They stared at each other for what seemed to Rowan like an eternity. Finally, her father turned to Rowan.

"I'm sorry, my dear," he had said, "Your mother and I are so proud of your skill with a bow and arrow. We are also proud of the young woman you are becoming. While it is one thing for you to challenge your brothers to contests of all kinds, it is quite another to engage young men not of the family in similar pursuits.

"We wish the world were different, so that we could allow you to compete against the young men," he continued, "but doing so would not be in your best interests."

"Why?" Rowan had shouted. "I'm better than most of them! Why can't I compete?"

Rowan's mother spoke.

"Society, even on Edanmore, where life is quite casual, has rules of polite behavior," she explained. "Girls do not compete against boys if they wish to be considered proper young ladies."

"I don't want to be a proper young lady!" objected Rowan. "I want to show them that I'm a great archer!"

"Yes, my sweet," said her father calmly. "We understand. We must all think about what is proper for the barony, not only for our own desires."

Rowan had not exactly rolled her eyes at this often-repeated excuse. Her defiant stance, with her hands on her hips, showed what she thought of this. Her father continued.

"We know that this is a disappointment for you, Rowan, but we know that you will obey us. Because you are a good and thoughtful young lady, your mother and I would like to offer you a boon."

Rowan's ears pricked up. A boon was the phrase her father used for what other people might call a bribe. She had learned that phrase early on when she had discovered that her brothers had many secrets they wished to conceal from their parents.

No one knew about Rowan's clandestine operations, which included listening at doors, peering through peepholes and looking innocent and unaware when adults were speaking. A girl in a family of boys had to use all her wits and skills to know what was going on around her.

One day, she asked her youngest brother Bertram why all the boys living at home sneaked back to their rooms early in the morning. He didn't explain. He had given her a penny not to tell their parents. That was the day that Rowan had become a spy and boon-seeker extraordinaire.

"What kind of boon?" Rowan asked carefully.

Her parents exchanged another one of their odd looks. Then her father continued.

"How would you like to learn to use a pistol?" he asked.

A boon indeed! Rowan had been trying to get her parents to get her a pistol and teach her to use it for over a year. She didn't want to hunt or kill things. She just wanted to learn how to use it and how to hit a target, like in archery. Rowan loved mechanical things of all kinds. she knew that she couldn't give in too easily.

"What kind of pistol?" she asked.
Her mother laughed.

"A lady's pistol made by Manton and designed especially for you," replied her father. "Would that be appropriate recompense for not competing against the boys?"
Rowan thought about it. She was fairly certain that none of the boys could shoot a pistol. And she knew, from listening to her brothers, that Manton's made the best pistols to be had.

"Who would teach me how to use the pistol and shoot it?" she asked skeptically.

Her mother answered.

"Your father, of course," she said, knowing that this would surely gain Rowan's agreement. With so many children in the house, and with her father's many business interests, time alone with him was a rare treat.

Rowan spit on her hand as she had seen her brothers do to seal a bargain. Then she extended her hand to her father.

The baron, to his credit, spit on his hand and shook his eldest daughter's hand, smiling. Rowan didn't see the look of both triumph and concern that her parents shared as her father shook her hand.

Since that day nine years ago, she had learned how to shoot not only pistols, but various types of rifles. She had also become an excellent fencer, and was very proficient with the use of knives. A gentleman from the Far East, who had spent some time at the castle, had, with the approval of her parents, taught all his daughters a type of fighting technique that enabled them to use leverage rather than strength to defend themselves. Rowan enjoyed this discipline and practiced it every day.

Her dream began to make sense. Rowan remembered the Summer Festival the year she turned sixteen. A dance floor had been erected in the courtyard of the castle, and the orchestra was tuning its instruments. Rowan was standing with her parents and greeting their guests. The Martins, a wealthy couple from town who were in the boat-building business, stepped forward with their youngest son, Adrian, who had just come down from Oxford.

Rowan had known the tall, pleasant young man with black curls, blue eyes and a quick smile, all her life. She was pleased to see him. She had no romantic interest in him. She had always thought of him as a brother. Then Adrian stepped back and introduced his friend, William Sutton, the second son of Viscount Willoughby. William had come down from Oxford with Adrian for a few weeks before heading back to school.

William Sutton was a striking blond young man. He was well over 6 feet tall, with a body that was honed to athletic perfection. His thick, lustrous golden blond hair was pulled back with a simple black leather tie. He had striking brown eyes with a twinkle of green, and his smile was easy and welcoming. Rowan was instantly infatuated with him. She'd never felt this way before. When he bowed over her hand and very properly kissed the air above her new white kid glove, her stomach suddenly felt like it was full of butterflies.

William was polite to all the young ladies, but he danced twice with Rowan. At the end of the evening, he asked for permission to call on her the next day. With her parents' consent, Rowan replied that she would be very pleased to receive him. She floated up to her bedroom, carried away with girlish dreams of love and marriage.

Every day after that, William and Rowan, escorted by one of the maids from the castle, roamed Edanmore. Some days they rode. On other days, they sailed or walked the hills. They talked about everything. William told Rowan about his plans for his future. He hoped to serve England as a diplomat. Rowan told William of her dreams of travel and for a home and children of her own.

Once in a while, on the rare occasions when they could slip away alone, William would steal a kiss. At first, his kisses were chaste and restrained, but as the days passed, his embraces become more enticing and fervent.

Rowan had never been kissed before. None of the boys on Edanmore would dare to embrace the baron's eldest daughter. William did not seem to be restrained by Rowan's status or her father's position.

William's kisses and touches awakened new feelings in her. They pushed her into a state of constant inexplicable tension. She floated through the days, wondering when he would kiss her and touch her again. At night, in her bed, she relived every touch of his hands, and every caress of his lips. She touched herself the way he had touched her, and imagined that her hands and fingers were his. She ached and burned for him.

On one memorable occasion, William had knelt before her, raised her skirts and kissed her most private parts! It had been both terrifying and unbearably exciting.

How could she forget the day when he took her hand and brought it to his solid member. As he had moved her hand along its length, he had whispered in her ear, "This is Willie. He wants you! He wants to nestle into your sweet, wet honey pot and fill you with delight."

Rowan's feelings were so strong, she almost fainted. He kept moving her hand against his rod until he shuddered and went still. "I've never had a woman touch me this way before," he said. "If only we could be one."

"If only we could be one," thought Rowan. "He wants to marry me!"

One evening, after this had been going on for several weeks, Rowan's parents asked her to join them in the study after dinner.

"Well, my Rowan," her father said. "Tell me about this young man you've been seeing. Are your feelings engaged, or are you merely enjoying his company while he visits the island?"

"I love him with all my heart!" Rowan replied. "I know that we're both young, but if he asked, I would happily marry him! He's kind and gentle and he wants to see the world and do wonderful things! I would love to do those things with him!"

"Are you sure?" asked her mother. "You haven't met many young men and your come out is at least two years away. Perhaps you'd like to go up to London next spring, see the sights and attend a few parties?"

Rowan smiled at her mother. "I believe I love him, mama," she said. "And I believe that he loves me. He is all that is caring and kind." Rowan's parents exchanged a glance.

"Very well," said her father. "When he calls on you tomorrow, have him come to see me. I will talk to him about his prospects and his intentions."

Rowan hugged her father and then her mother. "Thank you both so much!" she said. "I know that we will be very happy together." William's words, "If only we could be one," were echoing in her heart.

The next day, Rowan's mother suggested that they go into town before William was expected to arrive. The baron wished to have all the time he needed to speak with him. Rowan agreed.

Mother and daughter had a lovely afternoon paying calls and enjoying an impromptu picnic on a promontory overlooking the ocean. It was close to the evening meal when they returned. The baron came out of his study to greet them and invited them inside. He closed the door carefully and returned to his desk.

"Well?" asked Rowan. "What did he say?"

All day she had been in a state of high anticipation, but had managed to keep her feelings in check. Now that she was with her father, she could no longer control those feelings.

Her father looked at her with his kind, bright blue eyes. They didn't appear as merry as they usually did.

"I'm very sorry, my dear," he said to Rowan. "William is engaged to be married to a young woman who is an heiress and the daughter of a close friend of his father's. The engagement is of long standing, and they don't expect to marry for several years. The wedding contract has been signed."

Rowan jumped up out of her chair.

"I don't believe it! He said that he wished we could be one! He, he, he kissed me! He caressed me! How could he do that if he was engaged to another woman?"

She started to pace her father's study, her back to him. She didn't see her father rise to his feet at her artless confession. She heard, rather than saw, her father's chair strike the wall as he pushed it back in anger.

"He touched you? He dared? I'll kill him! I'll chop him into tiny pieces so small even the fish won't be able to feed on them!"

Her father strode to the door, threw it open and bellowed for the butler.

"Mr. Harris!" he shouted. "Get my hunting rifle! There's a fox among the chickens!"

Rowan's mother strode over to her husband, hoping to restrain him. This outburst was uncharacteristic of the generally calm baron. But then, he had never before been faced with the possible ruin of one of his daughters.

"No guns my dear," she said, putting her hand on his right arm. She waved Mr. Harris away as he came running down the hall with a massive rifle. "Come sit down and let's talk about this, get a little more information. No need to go off half -cocked."

She pulled her husband back into the study and guided him to the sofa, sitting down beside him. She gestured for Rowan, who was shaken by her father's display of anger, to sit down across from them. Maintaining a strong hold on her husband's arm, Rowan's mother said kindly to her, "Did William do more than kiss you and touch parts of your body, my love?"

It was not her father's shouting, but her mother's loving tone that made Rowan realize she was in serious trouble. But what did her mother mean by "more?" Ever an honest young woman, Rowan replied, "I don't know what you mean." Rowan's mother flushed a bright pink and said softly, leaning forward toward her daughter,
"Did he put any part of his body other than perhaps his fingers or his tongue, into your private parts?"
This time it was Rowan who jumped out of her chair, the color rising to her cheeks.

"Of course not! William would never do such a thing, would never suggest such a thing!" she retorted, although somewhere in the back of her mind she remembered his whispering the words
"sweet wet honey pot," and the feeling of his hard rod under her hand. Was it possible that William had wanted to do what her mother had suggested?

Rowan heard her father mutter angrily, and her mother whisper something soothing. This went on for several minutes while, deeply agitated, Rowan paced around the room. Finally she faced her parents and said, "How could he be so nice to me while he's engaged to another woman? I thought he loved me! I thought he wanted to marry me! If I knew he was engaged, I would have never walked out with him or have allowed him to kiss me! Oh, dear God! What am I going to do? Am I ruined?" She began to cry.

It was her father who walked over to her and pulled her into his arms.

"Hush, my dear, dear child. You are not ruined. Your heart is a little bruised. I know that your nature is pure and sweet. Never change. There are people in the world who may try to take advantage of your goodness, but you'll learn how to protect yourself as you grow in age and experience. Your mother and I will help you.

"None of us saw this coming. No one on Edanmore would dare to trifle with anyone in this household, but he was an outsider. He caught us all unawares. It may be time to expose you and your sisters to the outside world a little more. And perhaps, when you are ready, you will even tell your sisters this story, so that they will be a little more aware of the dangers that can spring upon a young woman."

Rowan hugged her father and nodded her head.

"But father," she said, "my heart is breaking! How will I bear it? I thought I loved him. I thought he loved me. I could imagine our future together, going all around the world with our children, and seeing all the strange and interesting people and places."

Rowan's mother came to her side.

"I know that it doesn't feel like it now, my dearest," she said, "but your heart will mend in time. What you feel is real, and that is a good thing. It means that, someday, you will love someone who will love you. For now, we will all help you while your heart heals."

The baron looked at his beloved wife over the head of their eldest daughter.

"Something must be done! There must be punishment for this terrible injury," his look said. "We will talk and consider what to do later," her gaze replied.

Rowan's mother took her daughter to her bedroom and tucked her into bed as she hadn't done since Rowan was a little girl. Rowan found this oddly comforting. The next morning, her mother brought hot chocolate and cinnamon buttered toast to Rowan while she was still in bed. While she helped Rowan wash and dress for the day, her mother told her their plans.

All the ladies, her mother told her, meaning Rowan, her two sisters and she, were going to go on an outing to the mainland and shop for new dresses. They were going to stay in a lovely inn overnight, do some more shopping the next day and then return home. It was time, Rowan's mother said, to get off the island and see the broader world.

She and the baron had decided that the girls needed to do some traveling. They were planning several longer trips, later in the year, and perhaps a trip to Dublin in the spring. Rowan's mother called a maid to help Rowan pack, and then went to roust her younger daughters out of bed to give them the good news.

The excursion, which Rowan had privately dubbed "the heartbreak journey," was a success. It helped her began to put her brush with ruination in some perspective. Leaving Edanmore with her mother and sisters was a new experience. When she returned home, she felt older and wiser.

Rowan had eventually shared the details of her experience with her younger sisters. Both Willow and Ivy swore to never fall instantly in love with anyone — although Ivy thought that it might be alright to fall instantly in love with a puppy with sweet brown eyes.

When the party returned home, the baron pulled Rowan aside.

"He's gone," he told her. There was no reason to say who "he" was. "I gave him a stern reprimand. I told him that I had already written to his father about his trifling with my daughter. I also warned him that if he ever referred to this incident again, or even permitted your name to pass his lips, I would hear of it. Then I would come after him and shoot him without a qualm. He believed me, because if he ever said one word that might cast aspersions against your good name, I really would have to dispose of the vermin!"

"Oh father," said Rowan, hugging him. "But am I not already ruined? I permitted a man to whom I was not engaged to touch me! To kiss me!"

"Bah!" replied her father. "Your mother and I don't socialize in London because of that sort of nonsense! You are an innocent young girl who was preyed upon by a handsome, more experienced young man. It's a story as old as time. If anyone is to blame, other than William, it is your mother and me. We didn't see the danger he represented, because we live in a place where no one would dare to harm any of my children. We let you wander as you always do. It didn't occur to us that he would take advantage of your freedom.

"You've had a little experience of love and passion without lasting results. I promise that your heart will heal in time. And when next you meet a man who catches your fancy, you will be more cautious, and have a better sense of how to go on. It's clear that it's time to think about how to prevent this from happening again. Your mother and I will take better care of all of you. That is a solemn vow."

Despite her parents' reassurances, Rowan was heartsick for many months, refusing to join her sisters for outings. There were even days, when she refused to leave her bedroom. Food had no interest for her and she lost weight. She refused her sisters' invitations to go riding with them. Her hair lost its luster.

Every night when Rowan went to sleep, she dreamed of William. She would ask him, "Why didn't you tell me you were engaged?" and he would respond, "I don't love her, I love you! I would do anything if only we could be together!" Then, in her dream, they would kiss, long, drugging kisses, and he would hug her and hold her tight. After a long time, she would begin to feel him being pulled away from her. She would try to hold onto him, but the force pulling him away was too strong. She would awake every night screaming, "No!" as tears ran down her cheeks.

Whatever else happened in her dreams, they always ended in this way, with her sweet William being torn from her arms, and her being unable to stop him from being taken away from her.

Over time, she slowly began to resume her normal life, but she was never again the fearlessly trusting young girl she had been before William had entered her life. She thought of him as the snake who had entered the perfect garden that was Edanmore.

Over the six years that followed, the dream occurred less and less frequently. The intensity of the loss that she experienced with each dream did not seem to diminish. Even in the heaven that was London and Edanmore House, she continued to dream of her lost love. Oh! How she wished that she was heart whole. How would she ever again be able to trust a man enough to love and marry him?

*"You must see what is going on outside
our home!"*

# CHAPTER FOUR
## *So Many Men!*
## *So Little Time!*

*Young men are like dogs with a bone. What one has,*
*they all desire. To find true love, look for the man who walks*
*away from the fray.*

*— Lady X's Admonitions to Young Women (Third Edition, 1802)*

The siege of Edanmore House began early the following
morning. Morning calls in town normally began at 1 o'clock
in the afternoon. Gentlemen decked out in the finest reflection
of their valets' art, began to form a queue outside Edanmore
House at about 11 o'clock in the morning. Many bore
elaborate floral tributes. Others carried boxes or packages
of various sizes.

It being at least an hour before anyone in polite society would accept a call, none of the gentlemen had the temerity to knock on the door. They just stood there, chatting with one another as the number of supplicants for the young ladies' notice grew longer by the minute. Mr. Harris, the butler, who had traveled with the family from Edanmore, noting the growing line, went to consult the baroness as to her wishes regarding her daughters' suitors.

The baroness was breaking her fast with her daughters in the breakfast room. As the room was in the back of the house overlooking Edanmore House's extensive park, the four women were unaware of the impending crisis. When informed that the cream of male London society had beaten a pathway to her door, the baroness laughed.

"Well, my dears," she said to her daughters. "The circus continues! What shall we do? I don't think that Madame Laval, even in her wildest flights of fancy, could have imagined this! I do believe that we should consult your father!"

The butler, the fifth generation of his family to serve the Higbees, was extremely savvy. He had already alerted the baron, about the situation brewing at his door. As the baroness was finishing her tea, husband walked through the door of the breakfast room.

"My dears," he said, addressing all of his favorite women, "you must come with me and see what is going on outside our home!"

"He's smiling," thought Rowan. "That's a good sign."

He led his wife and daughters to a small room they hadn't previously known existed. It was accessed through a hidden door in the parlor and was just large enough for six people to occupy with a modicum of comfort. Built into the outer wall was a viewing area that was undetectable from the outside. The viewing area permitted someone inside the room to see the entire entranceway to Edanmore House.

The four women looked around the room in amazement.

"When was this built?" asked the baroness.

"It's new," said the baron. "I asked Brian to create some safe rooms and some hidey holes while he was renovating. I've always been fond of them, and it will be such fun for the grandchildren when they visit us! Brian thought that this room would make it possible for us to decide whether or not we are at home to visitors depending on who we see on our doorstep."

Rose laughed. "My dear," she said, "you never cease to amaze me! This is truly a stroke of genius. But what are we going to do with all those gentlemen who are besieging our castle?"

"What would you like to do?" asked her husband, knowing that his Rose, wonderful strategist that she was, would have already imagined just this scenario.

"This is just so silly!" said Ivy. "I feel like I'm on display, like those poor creatures we saw at the Exeter 'Change. The Exeter 'Change, a menagerie built on the site of Exeter House on the north side of the Strand, competed with the Royal Menagerie to display exotic animals for the edification and entertainment of visitors. "I think that Harris should go out and tell them all to go away!"

Willow spoke up.

"I propose that we charge them each a shilling to gain entrance to the house. We can each give small groups of men a tour of the public rooms and then dismiss all but the ones we like most," she said.

They all laughed.

"That would certainly give us a nice little addition to our pin money," said Ivy.

"Perhaps we should see if there is a journalist present. Such a gathering of gentlemen would surely draw the notice of the press," said their mother. "We could invite the journalist in to speak with us. It is always advisable to have friends in the press. Perhaps he would be willing to mention in his story that we will only be at home on Mondays and Thursdays between 1 and 3."

"Do you really think there is a reporter out there?" asked Ivy.

"If you were a reporter, wouldn't you be out there?" asked Willow

"You know that he'll want interviews with all of you," said their mother. "Are you willing to do that?"

The three girls looked at one another and then at their father.

"It's fine with me," said the baron. "I agree that such a story will spread the news of our visiting hours almost as quickly as backdoor gossip."

"What do you think, girls?" asked the baron. "If you wish to speak with the journalist, your mother and I will, of course, be present to make sure that he doesn't overstep."

"Yes," said Rowan.

"Yes," said Willow.

"I suppose it will be alright," said Ivy, "but he'd best not get impertinent with me!"

They all laughed.

They all left the hidden room and settled in the parlor.

Then the baron went to the doorway, signaled to the butler, and gave him his instructions.

When the butler stepped out of the house, all the chattering stopped. All eyes looked up at him. In a well-modulated voice he said, "If there is a representative of the press, would he please step forward. The chattering began again in earnest. Why was a reporter being singled out?

A neatly dressed young woman in a dark blue day dress briskly walked up to the butler. The men in line immediately stopped talking, wanting to hear every word.

"I am S. J. Roberts," she said, her voice indicating that she had been well educated. "I am the society journalist for *The Ton Reporter*. How may I be of assistance?"

Harris had not been a butler for more than 40 years without learning how to deal with unforeseen circumstances. He nodded to the young woman and said, "The baron would like a word with you."

The reporter might have been relatively new to her career, but she knew an opportunity for a story when it presented itself. She smiled kindly at the butler and acknowledged his bow with a slight curtsey and a tilt of her head.

"It would be my pleasure," she said. She followed Harris into Edanmore House. As the door closed, a great deal of chatter erupted from the waiting swains.

S. J. was escorted up a broad, sweeping white marble staircase to the first floor of the massive building that was Edanmore House. The butler opened the door to one of the rooms and announced, "Miss S. J. Roberts of *The Ton Reporter*." S. J. walked into the room and took a moment to survey it, furiously making mental notes to add to her story.

She had been admitted to what must be the family parlor, she realized. It had a sense of coziness about it. She noticed an embroidery frame lying on a beautiful rosewood side table as though it had been just set aside. In a corner, tucked away but not quite out of sight, was a basket of what appeared to be children's toys. She had researched the Higbee family prior to their arrival in London. She knew that there were no children living at Edanmore House, although there were a great many grandchildren.

As she stepped into the room, an older red-haired woman with bright blue eyes, was walking forward to greet her. Obviously, the baroness, thought S. J. The other inhabitants of the room, a distinguished older man, presumably the baron, and three stunning young women, the daughters, judging by their marked resemblance to the older couple, all stood to welcome her.

"My dear Miss Roberts," said the woman, smiling, as she came up to S. J. and grabbed her right hand. "What an extremely delightful surprise! Welcome to Edanmore House. I am Lady Edanmore." Drawing S. J. into the room, Lady Edanmore continued her flow of chatter.

"May I present to you my husband, Baron Edanmore, and my daughters, Miss Higbee, Rowan to her intimates, Miss Willow and Miss Ivy.

S. J. curtsied gracefully and said, "It is a very great pleasure to meet all of you." Rising from her curtsey, she continued, "How may I be of service?"

The baroness led S. J. to a graceful armchair. The back and cushion were covered in a slightly faded but none the less exquisite needlework design. The baroness saw S. J. take note of the chair's covering.

"My husband's great grandmother, the wife of the sixth baron, did that needlework while in her first confinement," she explained. "She was a skilled needlewoman and a true artist. She and her husband were happily married and had eight children. There are seven other chairs covered in what has come to be called, 'confinement needlework' in our family. They are all singularly lovely and such a wonderful link to the past."

S. J. smiled. "What a lovely woman," she thought."

A beautifully dressed maid and several equally well-dressed footmen entered the room carrying a tea service and platters of sandwiches and cakes. They set up the tea table. The baroness poured out, inquiring as to S. J.'s preferences, and handed her a cup of tea and a plate with several tea sandwiches and a slice of cake.

S. J. observed the ritual with appreciation. The Edanmore barony might have been founded on an obscure island in the Celtic Sea, but the baron and baroness were obviously well-versed in the ways of polite English society.

S. J. thanked the patron saint of reporters for making it possible for her to infiltrate Almacks on the evening of the Higbee sisters' debut. The riot at Almacks had been quite something to behold. S. J. had managed to infiltrate that bastion of upper-class privilege with the help of a friend who assisted in the catering. She had been there to witness — and write about — the melée.

Some of her best stories had been obtained in a similar fashion. If one wished to make a name for oneself in journalism, such skulking about was absolutely necessary.

Indeed, she wondered why the baron and baroness were treating her as though she was an honored guest. True, the circumstances of her birth, she was the daughter of a marquis, gave her a higher social status than her hosts if it were to be known, she worked for her living. This should, by the rules of society, put her below their notice. Normally, a journalist, if acknowledged at all, would be greeted in a parlor set aside for tradespeople. To welcome her into their most private family space and treat her as an equal was extraordinary. "I wonder what they want?" she thought to herself. As she finished her tea, she believed that she was about to find out.

The baron stood and addressed her.

"Miss Roberts," he said, "You are probably wondering why we invited you to join us for tea."

S. J. smiled and nodded in the affirmative.

"We find ourselves in an interesting situation," he continued. "While it is true that all three of my daughters are making their debuts in hopes of finding husbands, we did not truly understand the effect of having all three of them come out at once. May I assume that you were at Almacks last night and wrote the piece in *The Ton Reporter* that we read this morning?"

S. J. smiled again and nodded.

"Very nice piece of writing," he said. "We were unprepared for the hordes to descend upon us in quite this way." He nodded towards the window. Although one could not see the line of hopeful suitors extending down the street, his meaning was clear.

"We would like to use you to mitigate the situation somewhat. We would be happy to give you something in exchange. We propose to give you the exclusive opportunity to interview our daughters, and to write about them in *The Ton Reporter*. In exchange, we would appreciate it, if you would include in your article, or articles, information about the days and hours that we will be at home to male visitors. In addition, there are some other details about the disposition of funds, dowries and that sort of thing that we would like you to incorporate into your story.

"My wife and I wish our daughters to marry for love. To discourage fortune hunters, we have set very low dowries for our daughters. On their marriage, each of our daughters will receive 1,000 pounds as a dowry. Any inheritance of funds or property other than that, will be wrapped up so tightly in legal instruments, that their husbands will never be able to gain access to that wealth.

"My wife and I are very determined about this. We would like the gentlemen of the ton to be aware of these arrangements. We suspect that at least half the men hoping for entrance today, will go on to greener pastures once they have received this news. What do you say?"

S. J.'s brain was buzzing. Of course, she would accept the baron's offer. An exclusive interview with the three most desired ladies of the season would be a major accomplishment. To accept without asking for something else, something more, offended her journalistic instincts. She looked at the three girls and at their parents. Then she knew how to respond.

"My lord," she began, "I am extremely honored that you have offered me, what I am sure you understand would be any journalist's dream. I also understand, that you did not select me over other candidates. Your butler asked to see the journalist and I stepped forward. I was clearly not what he, nor you, were expecting.

"That being said, I wish to thank you for the gracious way that you have received me. You welcomed me into your family parlor, and treated me as an honored guest. I would be delighted to have the privilege of interviewing your lovely daughters.

"I feel no qualms about adding such information as would serve to drive off fortune hunters, or anything else that you feel would add to the success of your daughters' season. I would like to make two requests.

"If you will permit it, I would like to do individual stories about your daughters. In addition, I am hoping that you will allow me to do a separate piece about you and Lady Edanmore. Since this is your first appearance in London in many years, you are news. Everyone wishes to know more about you and about the barony. Would you be willing to speak with me about yourselves?

"Let me say, before you answer, that if you do not wish to agree to these suggestions, I will still be happy to write an article about your daughters, and include any information that you feel is pertinent to their happiness."

The baron and his lady exchanged a long, silent communication. The baroness had a certain twinkle in her eye. Her husband knew that "twinkle" very well. His wife's marital hunting instincts had been aroused by the ease with which S. J. had navigated the tea ritual. The baron had previously noted her educated diction and accent. He was not a gambler, but the baron would have bet a good deal of money, that by the time the baroness had done her work, S. J. Roberts, reporter, would be good and truly married to a man of her own rank, one worthy of a woman of spirit and determination.

The baroness spoke.

"The baron and I would be very happy to speak with you about our life on Edanmore. We are very proud of the work done by previous generations to make life happy for all the island's citizens. We feel privileged to carry on those efforts. As for our daughters? What do you think, girls?" she asked, directing this last comment to the three young ladies who had been silent until now.

All three girls smiled and nodded. Rowan spoke for them.

"We would be happy to speak with Miss Roberts," she said.

"If I may make a suggestion, my lady," said S. J. "Those men who are lined up won't go away without having offered their tributes to your daughters, and being introduced to them. Instead of having them come into a parlor, a receiving line might be set up in the entrance way. Let them come in, be introduced to both of you, and your daughters, let them present their cards and offerings and then let them be shown out."

The baroness smiled. "That will show our good will, while sending the message that we won't be overrun. You could write a story about the receiving line, and include our visiting days and hours in the same story. For publication in tomorrow's paper, perhaps?"

"I would be delighted to do so," replied S. J. "And might I come tomorrow in the early afternoon to interview you and the baron? I think it would be proper to publish a story about the family background of your daughters, before the pieces about them appear."

The baron laughed.

"My dear," he said to S. J., "You are as gifted a strategist as you are a writer. Have you met Madame Laval? I think that you and she would get along very nicely."

"You honor me, my lord," replied S. J.

As they were talking, the baroness had gone to the door and had instructed the butler to set up the receiving line in the entranceway. She turned back into the room and said, "Shall we? The sooner we meet the ravening hordes, the sooner we can get on with our day."

**The next day.**

***The Ton Reporter — Friday Edition***
***A report by S. J. Roberts***

*The fascination with the lovely Higbee sisters continues, dear reader. Yesterday, after their epic appearance at Almacks, a queue of hopeful suitors began to assemble as early as 11 of the clock in front of Edanmore House, the stately mansion near Saint James's Palace. Edanmore House is the hereditary London seat of the Edanmore barony. By 1 o'clock in the afternoon, truly, quite early for a morning call, over one hundred gentlemen were lined up with lavish bouquets, boxes of chocolates, copies of the most recently published offerings by the Minerva Press, and reams of original poetry.*

*At 1:30, Mr. Harris, the distinguished butler to the Edanmore barony, opened the front door. He stepped outside and in a well-modulated baritone voice, explained that, upon presenting their cards, the gentlemen would be introduced to the entire family. They could then present their offerings. He went on to say, that after being introduced, the gentlemen were to leave.*

Mr. Harris asked the first five men in line to step forward. Taking their cards, he ushered them into the hallway, where the baron and baroness and their three lovely daughters were assembled to meet the gentlemen.

The gentlemen presented their offerings, which were then passed on to waiting footmen. Those with some ton bronze, presented a floral offering to the baroness, rather than to her daughters. She appeared very pleased by these delicate attentions.

The introduction of the gentlemen took well over an hour. Mr. Harris was kind enough to share with this reporter, that 146 cards were presented. All of the gentlemen who had been waiting, were introduced. The family has requested that this reporter inform the dear reader that this courtesy will not be repeated.

The family will have visiting hours every Monday and Thursday from 1 to 3 of the clock without exception. No visitor will be admitted after 2:35 o'clock. Any gentleman who has been introduced, and who wishes to escort one of the young ladies for a walk, or a drive in the park, or to some other amusement, is encouraged to send a note of invitation to Edanmore House rather than to rely on making such an arrangement during visiting hours.

Dear reader, this looks to be a most exciting season! Watch this column for more news about the family of Baron Edanmore. An exclusive interview with the Baron and Lady Edanmore is coming very soon!

*" ... the next thing I knew, Cupid shot an arrow into my heart and all was lost!"*

# CHAPTER FIVE
## *Love Is a Mischief!*

*When love strikes a gentleman, especially a Rake or a Corinthian, he is apt to fall hard. Because he has dismissed the notion of love for most of his adult life, he will be especially bewildered. Be kind, young ladies. An otherwise sensible young man may be thrown into a maelstrom of panic and indecision.*

*Should he be in love with you, and should you be interested in encouraging his attentions, a gentle but firm hand, and great patience will be needed. My experience has shown that once he makes his declaration and is accepted, he will settle down and become an exemplary husband."*

*— Lady X's Admonitions to Young Women (Third Edition, 1802)*

"You're falling apart, Max," said Grey. "It's been a week since you first laid eyes on the chit and I swear, you're pining away! What the hell is wrong with you?"

Max sprang out of his bed, not caring that he was stark naked, and lunged at Grey, trying to get his hands around his friend's neck.

"Don't you dare call her a chit!" he shouted. "She's a goddess! She's an angel! She's too good for the likes of you and me!"

Grey fended off his friend's assault with ease, which was unusual. Generally, they were very well matched in hand-to-hand combat, with Max having a slight edge because of his extra inch or two in height. This morning, Max was obviously soused to the gills, and his coordination was suffering as a result. Grey pushed him back onto the bed.

"I swear, man! You're drunk! I've never seen you in such a state!" shouted Grey. "I repeat. What is going on? I haven't seen you since Almacks, and then this morning I get a note from your valet of all people, asking me to come around and see if I can drag you out of your inebriated slumber!"

"I'm in love, Grey," said Max, despairingly. "I, the rake of all rakes, the leading Corinthian of the ton, am besotted and entirely bewildered. How did this happen? One moment, we were standing in Almacks surveying the newest crop of lovelies, and the next thing I knew, Cupid shot an arrow into my heart, and all was lost!"

"I was there, old man," replied Grey. "I saw it happen. She looked at you and you were gone. But what's the problem? You're Lord Maximillian Francis Browning, Viscount Darby, heir to the 7th Earl of Bainbridge. You are wealthy in your own right. You have women of all ages plotting to trap you into marriage and, dare I say it, less-confining amorous activities. You've been considered the catch of every season since we came down from Cambridge."

"I can't get near her," replied Max. "That first day, after Almacks, I went to make a call at the proper time, and there were men lined up in front of Edanmore House for as far as the eye could see. Of course, I didn't join the band. Then that article came out announcing the family's visiting hours. I came an hour early, thinking to get to the front of the line, and it was the same thing. There were at least fifty men already assembled.

"I've been riding in the park at the appropriate times, but the Flame Sisters haven't been seen. I even wrote a note to the baron asking to meet Miss Rowan. I got a note from his secretary explaining that at the present time, Miss Rowan was not meeting any new gentlemen. I tell you, Grey, I'm beside myself! What if she meets someone before I can get to her? What if she falls in love with him? My life will be over!"

"So, your solution this week has been to drink yourself into a stupor?" asked Grey. "What do your handlers at the Admiralty think of their top spy being on a week-long drunk? Haven't they noticed that you're not on the job?"

"I sent them a note that I was on the trail of an important clue," said Max. "That's our code for 'Leave me alone.'"

"Do you want her or not?" asked Grey.

"Of course, I want her!" shouted Max. "What will I do if someone else gets her? My life will be ruined!"

"You already said that. But Max, old man, you haven't even said hello to her. How do you know that you and she will suit?"

"She looked into my soul, Grey," Max moaned. "She saw all of me, all at once, and she didn't flinch. I could see that she was as drawn to me as I am to her! But of course, she can't come to me. She doesn't know who I am, and I can't seem to get to her! It's as if an evil spirit is keeping us apart."

"You, who never believed in love," said Grey, "are not only hopelessly in love but also now believe in evil spirits? This is serious indeed!"

Grey went to the side of Max's bed and tugged on the bell pull. A minute later, Max's valet, Finn, entered by the side door. Grey addressed him.

"Finn, we need to get your master sobered up and ready to go to the Carlton's ball this evening. I will come by and pick him up after dinner. Please make sure he is sober and dressed in his finest evening garb. Tonight, he is going to make the acquaintance of the future Countess of Bainbridge."

"In that case, my lord," said Finn, "I will make sure that he is a credit to my skills."

Knowing that his friend was in the hands of an artist, Grey left to see what strings he might pull to make sure that his friend would have at least one dance with his chosen bride. His first stop was at the home of his godmother, Lady Carlton. It was from her that he had discovered that the Flame Sisters would be attending that evening's ball. He had agreed to attend even though he knew that his godmother was match making. She hoped that at one of these events, he would meet a suitable woman, settle down and begin to see to the continuation of the earldom.

Lady Carlton never missed an opportunity to remind Grey that the succession lay on his shoulders and that he wasn't getting any younger. After all, like his best friend Max, Grey was almost 30 years of age. Lord Richard Grey Birmingham, 9th Earl of Wellesly Glen assiduously avoided almost all of his godmother's entertainments, except for those which were the most socially important (to his godmother.) He truly loved her, but he was not yet ready to settle down.

Grey was shown into his godmother's parlor, a tastefully decorated room in which the colors cream and pink created a restful atmosphere. Grey couldn't help thinking that he looked very well against this background.

When all the opening civilities had been observed, Grey's godmother asked, "What brings you here so early in the day, my dear? If you have come to cry off from my ball this evening, I will be severely displeased with you!"

"Just the opposite," Grey reassured her. "I have come to ask for a favor. My friend, Lord Browning, to whom you were so good as to issue an invitation, is besotted with the Honourable Miss Rowan Higbee, but he has been unable to arrange an introduction to her. Could I prevail upon you to introduce him to her, and to recommend him as her partner for the first waltz and the supper waltz?"

His godmother laughed.

"Since it was announced that the Edanmore sisters' dance cards would be filled out by the hostess of any event they attend, I have been besieged by young men bearing flowers, candy and books of poetry! For me! I almost feel as though I am making my own come out! If my dear Harley, your godfather, were alive, we would have a good laugh together.

"I'm afraid that two waltzes are completely out of the question, my dear. I would be driven out of town if I were to show such preference for a particular gentleman. All the hostesses got together and decided that we would always keep the supper waltz-free. We want the young ladies to be able to bestow that favor a particular suitor, should they wish to do so. I am sure that Miss Higbee would be delighted to dance the supper waltz with Lord Browning.

"As for you, my dear, may I assign the first waltz to you with Miss Willow and the supper waltz with Miss Ivy? And I assume that you will make yourself obliging to all the other young ladies tonight who find themselves without a partner."

"In other words," thought Grey, "You will dance with all the wallflowers." Understanding that this was his price to pay for the favor he had asked, Grey politely consented. "May owes me one," thought Grey. "I will insist that he also partner the wallflowers."

That evening saw Max restored and looking the perfect young man about town. If his heart was beating twice as fast as usual, and if he felt as though he had swallowed a few dozen crickets that were racing around his stomach, perhaps this was only to be expected. After all, Max was about to meet his bride, the mother of his many future children. Would Miss Higbee consider producing an even dozen, he wondered.

As Max and Grey stood together on the side of Lady Carlton's ballroom waiting for his intended and her sisters to arrive, Max turned to his friend and said, "What if she decides she doesn't want me?"

"Don't be an ass, old man," said Grey. "You're handsome, wealthy, the heir to an earldom and you have all your own hair and teeth. You're also the Admiralty's most intrepid spy. What woman wouldn't want you?"

Just then, the Higbee sisters walked into the room. The three young women appearing en masse still created a sensation. To avoid trouble, some hostesses had gone so far as to request that the sisters enter their ballrooms one at a time at ten-minute intervals! A story in *The Ton Reporter* explained that the gently-raised Higbee sisters became distressed when young man fought over them. This seemed to have restored decorum to London's ballrooms.

When this story was read at the Edanmore House breakfast table, it caused great hilarity. The three young women were used to tussling with their brothers.

When the Higbee sisters entered Lady Carlton's ballroom, Max, who had arrived uncharacteristically early, stood as still as a marble statue and stared. How was it possible that the eldest Miss Higbee, his Rowan, had grown even more beautiful, more transcendent, during the time since he had last seen her?

Rowan was dressed in the green of a midsummer forest, but it was a green that kept shifting and changing. Every move she made brought completely new colors into the world. Her creamy complexion glowed with health and vitality. Her lips looked plump and soft, and had a luscious raspberry hue. Max felt a stirring in his groin. He found himself wondering if her nipples and lower lips would be that color. Wouldn't it be wonderful to discover the answer to that question!

Faintly, as if from far away, soft strains of music began to invade Max's consciousness and he became aware of someone pulling at his arm.

"We have to do our gentlemanly duty now, Max," a voice said. It was Grey. "You'll get to meet her before the supper

*Anarchy at Almacks* | 75

waltz, as I told you. Now we have to pay the piper by dancing with the ladies without partners. I used the term wallflowers with my godmother today, and she scolded me soundly. Come. We'll start at the wall furthest away from the Higbee sisters and work our way toward them. And remember, no slacking! You owe me." And so, the ball began.

The first waltz was the second dance on the program. Grey had made sure that Max was engaged for this dance. Then he crossed the room to claim Miss Willow. He knew, from the extensive interview with her in *The Ton Reporter*, that she was the middle of the three sisters, and especially interested in the healing arts, both herbal and traditional, and that she loved nature and animals.

As they danced, Grey became entranced with Miss Willow's silky pale orange gold hair, which she wore loosely pulled back. It seemed to float around her pale neck and shoulders. Her gown was a pale orange. She seemed to glow from within.

Willow was tall for a woman, noted Grey, and wiry. Dancing with her was like dancing with a woodland being, albeit a tall one. She exuded a kind of fey quality that seemed to suggest that, while she was in his arms, she was also somewhere else. It almost seemed like she heard otherworldly music.

Willow's hazel eyes, which were rimmed with the faintest suggestion of emeralds, shined with excitement. After Grey had swept her into an admittedly grand sweeping turn, she laughed.

"This is our first London ball," she confided to him. "After Almacks, both of my parents decided that the ton needed some time to calm down. We've been staying close to home for the last week, although mama permitted us to dress in our old clothes and visit Hatchards in order to get some books. We snuck out the back door and used one of the old, closed carriages!" She laughed.

"At home, on Edanmore," she continued, "no one pays any attention to us. This experience in London has proved rather disconcerting," she confessed. "We worry that we won't find our own true loves, if we can't meet gentlemen in more normal settings."

"How have your at homes been working out?" Grey asked.

"Dozens of men are still lining up at the door," she replied. "We admit them three at a time, but really, most of them are so silly! It's as if they are competing to bring us the most elaborate floral offerings, the most exotic gifts and the silliest poetry! One gentleman even brought us a small monkey to keep as a pet! Father wouldn't permit us to keep it! I was honestly relieved. Monkeys belong in the wild. They shouldn't be pets."

"The other day, father put his foot down and forbid our guests to read their literary offerings! Can you imagine? One of the young men thought that he was jesting and went on reading his ode to Ivy's shoulders. Father went to the door of the parlor and the next minute two footmen appeared. They carried the man out just he was about to reveal his rhyme for the word silken. I really wish they had waited a moment more. I would have liked to have heard what he had come up with, although the poem itself was truly dreadful."

"I notice that you refrained from mentioning the poet by name," said Grey.

"I would never do that!" replied Willow. "He was a sweet boy and doesn't deserve to be held up to ridicule. He was just being silly." She sighed. "They all seem so silly. Father said that he may have to place a notice in *The Ton Reporter*, or even in the Times, with a list of the things that our visitors may not do! I hope that he was jesting. He has a rather uncertain sense of humor."

Grey had an idea.

"Perhaps Viscount Darby and I could be of help to you and your sisters. Would your parents permit us to make up a party of perhaps ten young men and women to enjoy a picnic in Richmond Park? We could include several chaperones in the party. Perhaps one of your brothers and his wife would like to come."

"Oh! Lord Birmingham! What an absolutely wonderful idea! The weather has been lovely of late and our coachman, who is never wrong, says that the nice weather will continue for at least another week. I'm sure that my parents would agree."

At that moment, the music stopped and the couple stood still, smiling at one another.

"She really is quite lovely," thought Grey, "though not the girl for me," he thought, relieved. "I shall have to find someone very special for her," he concluded. "Only the absolutely right man will do."

As he escorted Willow back to her parents, he began to consider which of his friends he might invite to the picnic who would be a suitable parti for Miss Willow.

"Mother, father," she said as they found the baron and baroness. "Lord Birmingham has had the most wonderful idea!" She proceeded to explain the plan to journey to Richmond for a picnic. Her parents exchanged one of their silent looks.

"Thank you for your kindness to our girls," said the baroness. "A picnic in Richmond Park sounds like a lovely idea. We will discuss your invitation with our other daughters and write a response to you tomorrow."

Grey had hoped that he would have been given an affirmative answer immediately, but, he supposed, it was only right to discuss the invitation with Willow's sisters. He bowed and began to turn away when Miss Ivy arrived escorted by the gentleman who had partnered her for the first waltz.

A great howl erupted in Grey's soul as the cur bowed over Miss Ivy's hand and kissed the air above it. "Mine!" it said. "Mine." From somewhere very far away, Grey thought that he could hear Lady Carlton's musical laughter. "Caught at last!"

Summoning all his strength and reason, Grey restrained himself from lunging at the presuming bastard's neck and wringing the life out of the miscreant. He drew a deep breath and bowed to Miss Ivy, saying in his most debonair voice, "Until the supper waltz, my lady." Then he turned and walked to a group of young women without partners in order to choose one for the next set.

Ivy looked at Willow. "Did you see?" she asked her sister in an undertone.

Willow laughed with joy. "If a man ever looks at me the way Lord Birmingham just looked at you, I think I would tie him up and abscond with him without saying another word!" Ivy laughed.

"But what if we don't suit?" she asked.

"There will be time to find out before he throws you over his saddle and rides away with you," said Willow. And then the two sisters laughed with joy. The season was beginning to come into focus.

Max danced every set with a young lady who was not surrounded by young men eager to make her acquaintance. Each one was lovely or sweet or smart, but lacking in either social status or fortune. Each one would make some lucky man a perfectly fine wife.

"Dolts!" he thought. The young men of the ton looked for all the wrong qualities in a wife. Money and beauty were fine in a woman, but to spend one's life with her, qualities of character and intelligence would wear better than title or wealth.

Max was happy to note that, once he or Grey had danced with a young lady, some of the more sensible male guests had approached them and asked them to dance. Maybe he and Grey should go on a quest to launch ladies without partners, so that they could find true love. "Everyone should marry for love," he mused.

He looked around and saw Grey partnering an extremely young woman whose dancing left a great deal to be desired. The girl was very pretty, but she looked like she should still be in the schoolroom. She seemed terrified. Poor girl.

As the last few notes of the music drifted off into the air, Max bowed to his partner and returned her to her chaperone. His heart was beating out of his chest. The supper waltz was next. Finally, finally he would meet his own true love!

Admonishing himself to be calm and collected, he began to walk towards the rest of his life. He saw Lady Carlton approach the Higbee party and whisper in the baroness's ear. The baroness looked around and summoned her daughters.

Her husband signaled a footman and gave him instructions. The next thing Max knew, the entire Higbee family had left the ballroom! He made his way as quickly as possible to his hostess.

"My lady," said Max, "may I inquire as to why the Higbee family made such an abrupt departure?"

"I suppose I can tell you," said Lady Carlton. "Their son, Benedict, who was coming to help with his sisters' season, was in a very serious accident just about a mile from Edanmore House. He was badly injured. A passerby arranged for him to be taken to the house. A doctor has been called for, but the butler sent for the baron and the rest of the family. It seems it's quite serious."

"Is there anything that I can do?" Max asked.

Lady Carlton smiled sadly at him. "You are a good boy," she said. "I'm proud of you. You can let the other gentlemen, who were hoping for a dance with the baron's daughters, know what has happened." She reached into her reticule, pulled out a list and handed it to him. "Please ask them not to disturb the family. Right now, they need to have all their attention turned toward bringing young Benedict through this. And Lord Browning. You can tell them that they can pray. Prayer can often bring miracles that medical men cannot."

"Max retreated to his secret lair."

# CHAPTER SIX
## What Is a Lovelorn Spy to Do?

*The life of the ton is like a calm lake. On the surface,
all seems peaceful. Below the surface there is teeming life —
predators stalking their prey and creatures living out their
lives unaware of danger around them! Young ladies! Be
vigilant! Much of what you will encounter during the Season
may not be what it seems!*

*— Lady X's Admonitions to Young Women (Third Edition, 1802)*

**The Ton Reporter — Thursday Edition**
**Dashed Hopes**
*An exclusive report by S. J. Roberts*
 *The hearts of many worthy gentlemen were dashed last
night when the Flame Sisters were whisked away right before*

the supper dance at Lady C —'s ball. It was the first time since the riot at Almacks that the beautiful sisters had graced a ton ballroom. Gentlemen who had not yet had the privilege of an introduction had hoped to remedy that sad situation. Those with an invitation to the ball had been instructed to apply to Lady C — in advance for a place on the ladies' dance cards. Within hours of that announcement, the young ladies' cards had been completely filled except for the supper waltz, which was intentionally left open.

The three young women were once again fashion plates courtesy of Madame Celeste Laval's genius. The eldest Miss Higbee was dressed in a severely cut spring green peau de soie gown that appeared to ripple as she moved. She looked like a warrior queen, sovereign of all she surveyed.

Miss Willow Higbee wore a soft orange lamé gown that seemed to float around her tall, lithe figure. The dress was edged in the thinnest, most delicate pale cream lace around the hem and the edge of her dainty puffed sleeves. As she danced, it seemed as though she was lit from within with life and fire.

Miss Ivy Higbee, at 18, the youngest of the three beauties, wore a clinging soft white velvet confection that set off her diminutive but perfect figure, signature bright-red curls and sparkling green eyes. A narrow dark-green velvet ribbon flowed from the sides of her dress to meet in the back in a beautifully tied bow. The long ends of the ribbon were trimmed with tiny silver bells that tinkled charmingly when Miss Higbee danced.

Illustrations of these marvelous creations, supplied by Madame Laval by permission of Baron Edanmore, follow this article.

*What, dear reader, was the reason for the early departure of the young ladies and their parents? This reporter was given exclusive details of the terrible event!*

*Mr. Benedict Higbee, the baron's sixth son, was in a dreadful accident that occurred only a mile from Edanmore House. The renowned breeder and trainer of exceptional horseflesh, who lives in Newmarket, was on his way to visit his family to act as an escort to his sisters during their season.*

*He was driving a racing curricle. As he turned a corner, a drunken cab driver, who was racing his cattle and not watching where he was going, rammed the side of the curricle, pitching it over. Mr. Higbee was thrown clear of the vehicle, which was reduced to splinters! The frightened horse dragged the wreckage through the streets until it was stopped by an alert gentleman.*

*A passerby saw the incident and raced to Mr. Higbee's side to offer assistance. Mr. Higbee was able to identify himself before losing consciousness from shock and pain. The passerby stopped a cab and he and the driver were able to transfer Mr. Higbee to the vehicle, which then rushed him to Edanmore House. Once there, the butler, the estimable Mr. Harris, called for a doctor and sent a note to Lady C — to request the return of the family.*

*It was a long and anxious night. Early this morning, your reporter received word that Mr. Higbee is resting comfortably and is expected to make a full recovery.*

*Miss Willow also requested that a note be included in this report to reassure readers that the horse involved in the accident, though slightly lame, is also expected to make a full recovery.*

*The family has requested no visits be paid for the balance of this week. Anyone wishing to send tokens of their concern for Mr. Higbee's recovery, may send a note. Those who wish to send flowers or other tokens are asked to send these to the Foundling Hospital in Bloomsbury to brighten the spirits of those unfortunate children.*

Max finished reading the story and stared down at his congealing eggs. Of all the rotten luck! He'd been on a dark road to despair when Grey had pulled him out of it and arranged for him to have the supper waltz with his Rowan. He'd been so close! And now this! How was he ever going to get his real life started — that's how he thought of it now, his real life — if he couldn't even meet the girl? He looked down at several slices of limp bacon. They had no advice to offer.

Max was thoroughly disgusted with himself. He was a spy, for pity's sake! And pretty good at his job, according to his superiors at the Admiralty. He was used to taking charge of difficult situations, finding a solution, solving problems.

He'd spent three dangerous years in Paris, collecting information on a network of anti-royalist sympathizers seeking to overthrow the aristocracy in England as they had in France. His work had led to the capture of those individuals and had thwarted the plot on the life of the King. He'd won a major promotion for his work. Yet here he was, unable to facilitate a simple introduction to his future countess!

The problem, Max decided, was that he was thinking like a lovesick calf! He needed to start plotting like the master spy that he was. Abruptly, he pushed back his chair and marched out of the breakfast room. His heels made a military beat on the polished marble.

He went to his study, locked the door behind him, walked to a wall of books and pressed a hidden hinge. The bookcase slid open. Max entered his secret room and the door automatically closed behind him. Whenever he needed peace and solitude to work on a difficult problem, Max retreated to his secret lair. He had designed this room himself and had it built by specially-trained craftsmen who worked for certain government agencies who required gifted carpenters with a high level of discretion.

A large leather chair took up an entire corner of the small room. Next to it was a table that could be positioned in front of the chair to act as a desk. He lit two oil lamps, drew a small notebook from a shelf, and opened it to a fresh page. A sharpened pencil, a relatively new invention, lay on top of the table. Max found it to be more efficient than a quill and ink. How he loved new technology! He picked up the pencil and started to make a list.

"Steps to take," he wrote. Below that he wrote "1." Next to the number, he wrote the words "Higbee family engagements."

"Family engagements," thought Max. In order to meet Rowan, he needed to know where she might be on any particular day, at any particular time. It would be helpful if he could place a spy within the household, someone who could find out about the family's engagements and get that information.

Max sighed in frustration. Infiltrating a household was a delicate business. In a poorly run household where there was a great deal of staff turnover, placing someone inside was fairly easy. From some initial inquiries, Max had learned that the

Higbee establishment was a tightly run, and happy, ship. There didn't seem to be any turnover in staff. Most of their servants had been with the family for generations and were absolutely loyal. A new person would stick out like a sore thumb. Slipping a spy into Edanmore House was not an option.

Watching from the inside wouldn't work. What about surveillance from outside the house?

Perhaps he could set up some watchers outside and some messengers. As soon as Rowan was spotted leaving the house, a messenger could come to alert him. It wasn't the most sophisticated plan in the world, but it could work.

He'd need some help. Children were good for that type of task. Most adults didn't pay attention to children who were loitering on the street or playing games in a park. In the past, when he needed a young person's help, he had sent his butler to employ Timmo, the young boy who was the official street sweeper at the corner of Max's street. The young boy had been very reliable. Perhaps Max could recruit him again. Timmo probably had some friends who would also be willing to work for some extra coin. It wasn't a bad idea. He stood up, more hopeful than he had been in some time. He had a plan.

Max left his secret spy den and walked to the door of his study. He pulled the cord to summon Samuels, his butler. When that good man didn't instantly appear, he stuck his head out of the door and shouted for him.

"Samuels," he shouted.

When Max had set up his household, he had asked his father's retired butler, with whom he had grown up, to take charge of his London home. The man had declined the invitation, citing his age. He had suggested that Max might find his grandson, recently released from the army due to a slow-healing leg injury, to be a worthy successor.

The leg injury had left the grandson with a slight limp. The limp didn't seem to slow him down in the least. He was an excellent butler who ran the house with military precision. Despite this, the household staff exhibited an outstanding *esprit de corps* that was unusual in most households in London. The house ran like clockwork and its employees always seemed happy, well-clothed and well-fed.

In addition to his outstanding administrative abilities, Samuels was a man of unique talents. He had an uncanny knack for picking locks. He also had an odd genius for making all kinds of makeshift tools and contraptions. Because of his skills, Max had taken Samuels with him on several missions and had found him to be a resourceful aide as well as a pleasant companion. It was good to have someone in the house on whom he could rely.

"Sorry, my lord," Samuels said, breathing heavily as he entered the room. "I was working on a new gadget down in the basement and it took me a bit of time to disentangle myself."

Max waved his hand, indicating his understanding.

"Samuels," he said, "I'm working on a little problem and I could use Timmo's help. Would you please ask him to meet me in the kitchen for a short talk? Tell him that I'll give him something to eat and pay him for the loss of his street sweeping tips while he's talking with me. Bring him in through the kitchen door."

Ten minutes later, Max and Timmo were seated at the large wooden kitchen table with mugs of tea and a plate of sandwiches in front of them. They ate in companionable silence for a few minutes. After Timmo had eaten most of the sandwiches, he brushed his hands together and turned to Max.

"Thank you for the fine meal, yer lordship," said Timmo. "Me job at the corner 'elps me eat every day, but a little something extra is always welcome."

"It is my pleasure to have you as a guest at my table," said Max, recognizing the beginning of their business negotiations. He had forgotten that about Timmo. The boy was extremely smart and savvy.

"How can I 'elp yer lordship?" asked Timmo.

"I have a house that needs watching. It's quite nearby. The big house near Saint James's Palace. It's called Edanmore House."

"I know that 'ouse," said Timmo. "I liked to go past there when they was fixin' it up. Every once in a while they needed 'elp. I picked up good coin there. It's a big 'ouse with a lot o' doors. Watching that 'ouse is a six man job. Would yer want it watched day and night?"

Max smiled. The boy was good.

"I'd like it watched from right before dawn to when they either go out for the evening or when it is clear that they are staying in for the night," Max explained. "I would also like two messengers who could track me down as soon as the destination of a specific party is established. A particular young lady."

Timmo looked straight at Max, a frown on his face.

"Are yer plannin' to kidnap the mort?" he asked.

"Cockney slang," thought Max. "It's so colorful!" Then he responded to Timmo.

"Of course I'm not going to kidnap her. And she's no mort. She's a young lady of fine birth and blameless reputation." He said this with some heat.

"Then why are yer trackin' 'er?" asked Timmo.

"I need to meet her," Max explained. "For quite respectable purposes, I assure you," he hastened to add. The last thing he had expected was for Timmo to question the propriety of his own actions! The boy was a surprise.

"Who is she?" asked Timmo, "the one what needs watchin?"

"Have you heard of the Flame Sisters?" asked Max.

"Wot!" said Timmo. "The three young ladies with the red hair wot's been in the newspaper? Yer want I should watch them? Wot's the matter? Can't yer get close enough to meet 'em? Yer a bloody LORD for pity's sake! Yer rich! Why wouldn't they want to meet *you*?"

"It's complicated," said Max, somewhat abashed by the street sweeper's interrogation. "Do you want the job or not? It would be up to you to recruit the other young people and the messengers. Both girls and boys. I will pay each of you six pence a day for at least a week — seven days guaranteed — even if it turns out that I don't actually need you all for seven days."

Timmo was shaking his head. Max was puzzled. Did Timmo think that Max wasn't offering enough? Indeed, Max had been of a mind to pay a shilling a day, but thought that such a payment might make Timmo think that Max was up to no good. What was wrong with six pence a day? That was three and a half shillings for a week's work. It was a fortune for a child living on the street. They could have food and modest shelter for months.

"What's wrong, Timmo?" asked Max.

"How did you get to be so rich, throwin' blunt away like that?" asked Timmo. "Yer talkin' about a small fortune! Thruppence a day is more than enough, especially if yer willin' to supply some food at the beginning of the day and at the end of the day. It don't need ta be fancy. Just somethin' to put in the belly. An' some ot' water ta drink."

Max looked at Timmo assessingly.

"And what do you want for yourself?" he asked.

"The same as the others," Timmo said. "It would make them feel bad if I got more."

"This boy," thought Max, "is extraordinary. I've got to get him off the street, if he'll come, and see that he gets an education worthy of his intelligence. He could grow up to be Prime Minister!" That would have to wait.

"Four pence and not a penny less," said Max. "I insist. And everyone comes to the kitchen before starting in the morning for breakfast and tea, picks up a package of food at midday and comes back to the kitchen for a meal and tea at the end of the watch."

Timmo spit on his palm and held it out to Max.

"Yer drive a 'ard bargain, yer lordship," said Timmo, smiling.

Max spit in his palm and shook the boy's hand.

"If you can round up the gang by dinner time," he said, "bring them all here so that I can meet them and explain exactly what I want them to do."

"We'll be 'ere as soon as can be, yer lordship," said Timmo. He stood up and bowed to Max.

"Nice doin' business with yer, my lord," he said sincerely.

Watching the young boy leave, Max wondered where he had learned his manners. Here was an interesting puzzle to solve when the goal of making Rowan his bride had been achieved.

The next morning before sunrise, the watchers were in place around Edanmore House. Max had deputized Samuels to supervise Operation Rowan and alert him as soon as she and her sisters were on the move. The stables had been notified to have a mount ready for Max at a moment's notice. A footman was on standby to deliver a message to Grey so that he could rendezvous with Max as soon as they knew where their quarry was headed. After all, it wouldn't do any good to intercept the sisters if Grey wasn't on hand to make the introductions. He had, after all, danced with Miss Willow so it would be proper for him to introduce Max to Rowan. Every part of the plan was in place. Now all they had to do was wait.

Later that day, it started to rain. No one was seen leaving Edanmore house. The next day it rained. And the next. And the next. The family stayed home. As each day dawned, Max sank more deeply into a state of gloom. It continued to rain and the Flame Sisters and their parents stayed inside their London home, warm and dry.

Could it be that God had planned another 40-day deluge just to keep Max from meeting his true love? Had some evil witch cursed him at birth? Had he once cut down a sacred tree or somehow angered the Fates? Was Nature herself conspiring against Max's happily ever after?

The irony of a master spy being bested by Mother Nature was not lost on Max. If Mother Nature herself was conspiring against him, how would he ever meet his true love?

*"Determine what you must do to see your desires fulfilled!"*

# CHAPTER SEVEN
## *Fortune Favors the Bold!*

*Young ladies. Let me impart a secret to you! If you want to see your fondest dreams come true, you must take control of your lives! I know this is a radical idea! There are times when circumstances will not go as you wish. Should you find yourself in such a situation, do not linger, waiting for things to change. Instead, you must be deliberate in your actions. Determine what you must do to see your desires fulfilled! As the Good Book says "Be sober! Be vigilant!" Action, young ladies! Fortune favors the bold!*

*—Lady X's Admonitions to Young Women (Third Edition, 1802)*

"You look much better today, Benedict," said Willow to her beloved brother, who was reclining on an unusually-long chaise lounge in the family's sitting room.

"His eyes look brighter," chimed in Ivy, who had entered the room with her sister.

Benedict was comfortably ensconced on the well-padded piece of furniture supported by half a dozen embroidered pillows. He was stroking a dark grey kitten curled in his lap that was purring quite loudly for its diminutive size.

Truth be told, not much of Benedict's face could be seen. Willow had a tendency to be very liberal with bandages, especially for head and face injuries. Only the tip of his patrician nose, the circles of his brilliant green eyes and the curve of his full lips could be seen through the bandages Willow had applied. Benedict's gold-streaked auburn hair was covered with a cap of white bandages.

When the family had returned from Almacks on Wednesday night, the doctor had already examined Benedict and had pronounced him somewhat battered and bruised but otherwise unharmed. He had promised to come back the following day and to bleed him and use leeches if necessary. The doctor also left some laudanum for pain

Benedict was already asleep, so Willow didn't feel the need to wake him. On Thursday morning, she had insisted on performing her own examination. She had applied various poultices and bandages and also began to dose her brother with various herbal remedies. Such was the confidence of Willow's family in her healing skills that Benedict submitted without protest to her ministrations. It was now Friday afternoon and Benedict was getting restless with inactivity.

"That foul-tasting stuff that you and Ivy brewed and shoved down my throat is probably the reason I'm getting better," he replied.

Ivy laughed. Since she was old enough to toddle along after her elder sister, she had been Willow's assistant in the stillroom in their home on Edanmore Island. Although not a natural healer like Willow, Ivy enjoyed learning about how the combination of various ingredients could create different outcomes. It was like an endlessly changing puzzle and Ivy loved solving puzzles. She was particularly fascinated by poisons.

Benedict smiled at Ivy's laugh. Living in Newmarket, he didn't get to spend much time with his sisters. All three of them were delightful young women. Perhaps a few weeks here in London wouldn't be so bad. This thought brought his mind to a subject that he knew they would enjoy talking about.

"If it stops raining sometime today," said Benedict, "I think that we should be able to take the horses to the park on Sunday afternoon."

"That would be so wonderful!" replied Ivy joyfully. "I can't wait to ride that lovely white Arab mare you brought for me. I'll feel like a princess mounted on her."

Benedict chuckled. "You would look like a princess mounted on the lowliest donkey," he replied. "But I admit that when I saw that mare in a field near my stables, I knew that she would be just right for you!"

Ivy threw her arms gently around Benedict's neck.

"You are the best brother in all the world!" she cried.

Each one of them was dear to his heart. As if his thought had summoned her, Rowan entered the sitting room.

"I heard that mother had given her permission for you to walk down here and rest on the sofa," she said. "I wonder what the doctor would say?"

"The doctor!" spat Willow. "He wanted to bleed Benedict twice a day, put leeches all over his body and stuff him full of laudanum! The very idea! A healthy man like Benedict can recuperate by himself if given half a chance and the right herbs and nourishment. Bleeding! Leeches! It's positively medieval! And laudanum! That filthy stuff is responsible for so much pain in the world!"

"We heard you screeching all the way down the hall," said Rowan. "What did you do to drive the doctor away when he came on Thursday?"

"I treated him to a historic performance of the 'Witches Lament,' from the play we wrote for our Samhain celebration last year," said Willow. "The one where the witch throws herself on the floor and writhes in pain, tearing at her hair and at her skin while shouting obscenities at the top of her voice!"

"Willow Blair Higbee!" said Rowan, slightly shocked, "You didn't say all those words! You wouldn't!"

Willow laughed. "I shouted them in Gaelic! They sounded even worse!"

The three sisters laughed. Benedict shook his head.

"Don't encourage her!" said Benedict. "I could see what was happening and I couldn't believe it! The doctor was horrified! He raced from the room as fast as he was able. I don't think he'll ever call here again."

"As long as I'm here," said Willow, "we won't need him. And father can surely find a doctor for the family who has more modern ideas. I'll interview anyone he brings around to make sure that he leaves his instruments of torture where they belong, buried under a big mound of dirt!"

Benedict looked at his sisters and smiled. "I'm a very lucky man to have such wonderful sisters," he said.

Rowan smiled at her brother. He was such a handsome man. She wondered how he had been able to avoid being enticed into marriage. His muscular build was that of a horseman. Everyone liked Benedict and he seemed to be at ease with everyone he met.

"When some woman throws him to the ground, ties him up tight and drags him to the altar, she's going to be a very happy wife!" Rowan thought. Benedict insisted that he was a confirmed bachelor. So far he'd been able to slip through his stepmother's marital snares. She seemed to have given up on finding Benedict a wife.

Rowan and her sisters knew better. Their mother was just waiting for the right time to strike. She wouldn't be happy until all of her children, and that meant her stepsons as well as her daughters, were happily married and filling their nurseries! Let Benedict drift along in his bachelor fantasy, thought Rowan. Their mother would win in the end!

The door opened and their father walked in.

"How are you feeling, my boy?" he asked. "Are Willow and Ivy still plying you with noxious but healing remedies, or have they pronounced you fit?"

"Willow says that if I'm a very good boy and rest for the next two days, I can then go out for a short ride if it's not raining," said Benedict.

"Well, that's good news," replied his father. "If we don't let the gentlemen of the ton see my daughters soon, they may lay siege to Edanmore House. I received three more proposals of marriage this morning, one for each of my beauties. One is from a duke!"

"A duke?" responded Willow. "Which duke? Not the old one with the hair coming out of his ears who introduced himself to us even before we entered the ballroom at Almacks?"

"The very one," said the baron. "And he was especially smitten with you, my Ivy."

"Oh father, no! You wouldn't want me to marry that man! He's 80 if he's a day! He's been married four times and has dozens of children and grandchildren. They all live with him." He told me all about it! He told me that the long winters are why he has so many children. He leered at me!"

"He *is* a duke," her father said, "and a fairly wealthy one. Besides, how much longer can he live? You'd be a duchess! Just think of it!"

"No father! No! I won't marry that man, even to please you!" Ivy was getting agitated. "I love you like a daughter," she said, their on-going joke making her eyes sparkle, "but I can only marry for love!"

"Hush now, my love," said her father, gathering her into his arms. "I love you like a father," her father said, giving her the required response to their joke. "I'm just teasing a little bit. He isn't nearly good enough for you! I don't care who you marry as long as you love him and, he truly loves you. Besides, I would never give a positive response to any suitor without consulting my daughters first, said the baron, looking at Willow and Rowan. He smiled at them and gave Ivy a big hug.

"John Coachman says that the rain will stop in a day or so and that the ground should be dry enough in two days for you all to take your mounts to the park if you wish," continued their father. "I know that Benedict will be with you, but I think you should each take a groom just in case."

"A good idea," said Benedict. "I could protect any one of them, but three together might be a bit beyond me in my somewhat weakened state."

"That sounds like a good plan," said their father. He left the parlor.

"I can't wait to ride Moonbeam," said Ivy.

"Moonbeam?" said Benedict.

"That's what I've named her," replied Ivy. "I've been visiting her in the stable and talking to her. She's as bright as a moonbeam. She's also very sensible. And she likes me. I think we're going to be a wonderful team," Ivy said.

"Have you and Willow been visiting your mounts?" Benedict asked Rowan.

"Indeed, we have," said Rowan. "In fact, I know that you meant the black gelding for me and the bay stallion for Willow, but we've decided to switch. The gelding likes Willow better than he likes me, and the stallion has a very protective air towards me."

"And their names?" Benedict asked.

"Torin, for my gelding," said Willow, "because he sees himself as a leader of other horses, a chief, just like his name.

"And your stallion?" Benedict asked Rowan.

"Donn," said Rowan.

"Donn?" asked Benedict. "That means 'brown.' Couldn't you come up with something more creative?"

"I think it's a lovely name," said Rowan, smiling softly.

"Brownie, Brownie," teased Ivy in a sing song voice. Turning to Benedict, she explained, "Rowan's in love with Lord Browning."

"Lord Browning?" Benedict asked.

"Lord Maximillian Francis Browning, Viscount Darby, heir to the Earl of Bainbridge," said Willow without taking a breath. "His friends call him Max, she added helpfully. Rowan lovvvves him!"

"I don't lovvvve him," Rowan retorted. "We haven't even been formally introduced."

"But you saw him across a crowded room!" Ivy added. "Your eyes met! Your hearts became as one! You knew in that instant that you would be together forever and ever!" she proclaimed dramatically, drawing her hands together to her heart and pretending to faint to the floor.

"We've got to get her to read something other than those horrid gothic novels," Rowan commented to Willow. "They're driving her mad!"

Benedict laughed at Ivy's antics, but then turned his attention to Rowan.

"Do you really think that you might have a special connection to this Max fellow?" he asked seriously.

Rowan blushed.

"I think so, yes," she said. "Ivy wasn't completely wrong. We saw one another across the room at Almacks on the night of the riot. He started toward me, and then, well, you know what happened then."

"And have you seen him since then?" Benedict asked.

"We were supposed to have the supper waltz at Lady Carlton's ball," she said.

"And then I interfered with your plans," her brother commented. "So sorry about that. Had I known that you were going to meet your true love, I would have avoided getting into an accident."

Rowan walked over to him and slapped him lightly on the shoulder.

"Silly! You are so silly! I know I'll eventually meet Max, but what if he meets another woman before he meets me, and he falls in love with her?"

"Not going to happen!" said Benedict with a sense of absolute certainty."

"You can't say that," said Rowan. "You can't know that for sure."

"Ah," said her brother, "but I can."
Benedict tried to sit up straighter and he winced. He hated being unable to move easily. He continued.

"I'm going to arrange for you to meet your future husband in the next couple of days. I know how to make things happen! I make them happen all the time!"

"Really?" Rowan said. "You can really arrange for me to meet Max?"

"Easiest thing in the world!" responded her brother. "By the end of the week, you'll be planning your nuptials with him!"

"Oh, you are the very best brother in the world!" said Rowan, gently hugging him. "I really love you! Oh! If I'm going to meet him, I've got to make sure that my very best riding habit is ready! I'm not sure that Madame Laval delivered it! I have so much to do." She ran to the door and then looked back at her brother. "Oh! I really do love you!" cried Rowan as she dashed out the door taking her sisters with her.

Benedict stared at his sisters' backs as the door shut behind them. He closed his eyes. Why did he always do this to himself? How was he ever going to engineer a meeting with this Max fellow? He sighed. Then he had an idea!

*"Was this genuine, or was it a trap?"*

# CHAPTER EIGHT
## *The Best-Laid Plans ...*

*The men of the world would like to believe that ladies are mild, weak and retiring, needful of the protection of men. We, young ladies, know better. While it may profit one to affect such a charade to forward one's plans, never let pretense overpower your ability to take care of yourself, should the need arise. A strategic faint may be called for occasionally, but when in true danger, such a ploy could be fatal! When threatened, act to save yourself! Don't wait for your knight in shining armor to come riding to your rescue. For all you know, his horse may have come up lame!*

*— Lady X's Admonitions to Young Women (Third Edition, 1802)*

Max was just sitting down to dinner when Samuels brought him a note.

"The boy who brought it said that it was very important and that you should read it immediately," Samuels informed him.

"I guess I should read it immediately," said Max. He opened the message, which he noted was written on a piece of very fine paper.

*There is a very proper young lady who would like to make your acquaintance, the note began. There is reason to believe that you might also like to make her acquaintance," the note continued. If the weather is fine, the young lady will be riding a fine bay stallion in Hyde Park shortly after sunup two days hence in the company of her sisters, one of whom you have already met. Should you meet up with this party, an introduction will follow. A friend.*

Max stared at the note in his hand. Was this genuine or was it a trap of some sort? Who would write such a note to him? And could it possibly refer to an actual meeting, at last, with his future countess? Should he investigate further, or should he acquiesce to possible good fortune? Fortune favors the bold, he thought.

Max raced to his office, pulled out a piece of paper and quickly dashed off a note.

"Samuels," he shouted. When the butler appeared, Max said, "Please have this note delivered to Lord Birmingham immediately. Make sure that it is put into his own hand."

Samuels took the note, bowed and left the room.

"Finally," said Max, to the empty room, "I'm going to be united with my love. It will be the first step to making her mine."

Two mornings later, Max was up and dressed to impress even before the sun had risen. He hacked over to meet Grey at his town house. Grey looked very elegant mounted on his black stallion. Max was riding his favorite town horse, Sheik, a white Arabian gelding with a particularly flashy way of holding his neck and tail.

The two men made their way through the streets toward Hyde Park and Rotten Row. At the fashionable hour, it was the place to be seen, and one could only proceed at a sedate walk. In the early morning, the broad flat track was generally deserted and served as an excellent place to get in a good run. The track was about eight tenths of a mile, so several circuits were a fairly decently workout for town.

Rotten Row was deserted when the two men arrived. The first rays of the sun were just beginning to peek above the buildings surrounding the park.

"To the end and back?" suggested Grey.

"On the count of three," agreed Max. "One, two..." As he said "three," he urged his steed forward and put several feet between himself and his friend. The two horses were well matched. Max, by dint of his somewhat illegal start, won by a nose.

"I don't want to say that you cheated," said Grey, laughing. "Wouldn't want you to call me out," he continued, "although the Jockey Club might not have approved of that start, old man

"Do you see anyone from the Jockey Club here?" Max asked him, raising his right eyebrow. "Besides, that's a spy trick! Always get a jump on your opponent."

"A jump indeed," said Grey. "That mount of yours is really something special. I'd like to see what he could do in a fair race."

"Next time you come out to the country, we'll set something up," said Max. As he said that, he looked around. In the distance, he saw a party of riders approaching.

"If I'm not mistaken, that group is the Flame Sisters and their grooms," said Grey. "But who's the tall, well-dressed chap? I haven't seen him before. Could he be a suitor?"

"He's got the look of the Higbee boys about him," said Max. "Eight of them, you know. I've met Bertram Higbee. He's a very good solicitor. I was introduced to him at the club a few months ago. He recently married the Dowager Countess of Easton Grey. I heard that she's increasing. Fast work, if you ask me."

"Broderick Higbee-James was pointed out to me once when I was at my bank," Grey commented. "He's the one who's a genius with investments. I've been thinking of consulting him about my estate. And I caught sight of Brian Higbee, the architect who refurbished Edanmore House, one day when I walked past when they were still working on the exterior. The Higbee boys don't exactly look alike, but they all carry themselves with a certain air. As though they are happy in their lives and know their place in the world. Not arrogant, but comfortable in their own skins. It's an unusual quality. Quite compelling."

"If he's a Higbee, which one is he, do you think?" asked Max.

"Judging from the way he's communing with that dun stallion, as if they were part of a single whole," said Grey, "my guess is that he's the brother who has the stable in Newmarket. Benedict, I think his name is. Have you ever seen a man sit a horse like that? He looks like he's a centaur!"

"Impressive," Max agreed. "They're coming this way! I can't believe that I'm going to finally meet my Rowan!" Look at her! Isn't she the most elegant woman you've ever seen?" As the group drew closer, Max could see that Rowan was wearing a dark blue wool riding dress with a matching short jacket trimmed in gold braid. Gold buttons decorated the front of her jacket. The dark blue, military-style shako hat, decorated with thin gold braid, had the customary white feather attached to the front. She wore matching blue leather riding gloves.

Max thought he had never seen anything as adorable as his love in his entire life. Had he been offered a thousand pounds to describe what Rowan's sisters were wearing, he would have been utterly unable to do so. His astute powers of observation, which had saved his life more than once, had completely deserted him. He only had eyes for Rowan.

Only a minute or so more and Max would be introduced to the future countess of Bainbridge. He mentally inventoried how he looked. He reached up and straightened his hat. Was she as nervous as he? The writer of last night's anonymous letter had suggested that she wished to be introduced to him. But what if the letter had been a joke?

Suddenly, his heart dropped to the bottom of his highly-polished Hessians. He had never even considered that perhaps someone was playing a prank on him! What if his Rowan didn't want to meet him at all? What if he had been lured here to the park to be publicly humiliated when she gave him the cut direct! What if dozens of people were secreted behind trees, ready to reveal themselves and laugh at him! A cold shudder ran down his spine. He turned his attention from Rowan to ask Grey if he thought that this was all a prank.

At that moment, a shot rang out! In the quiet of the early morning, it sounded as loud as a cannon blast. Max turned toward the place where he thought the shot had come from. There was a grove of trees that would be perfect cover for a sniper. Instinctively, he started toward them. Grey called out to him.

"Max, over there! Look!"

The group of young ladies from Edanmore had responded to the shot, not by running away, as any well brought-up young ladies would do, but by galloping fearlessly toward the stand of trees! Their brother and the grooms were with them, trying to get them to turn back, but the three sisters seemed determined to discover the source of the gun shot and to capture the shooter! Were they mad?

Max changed direction and streaked toward Rowan, hoping to intercept her before she reached the trees. The sniper might still be there, waiting to get off another shot!

Rowan was slightly in front of her sisters, riding full out on her bay stallion. Some odd, detached part of Max's brain, noticed that the horse was as fine a mount as he had ever seen. He had to get to her, to save her!

Sheik was a horse that was all heart. He understood that his mission was to run down the large bay stallion. He stretched out into a ground-eating gallop and drew nearer and nearer to the fine bay. As he drew up beside him, Max reached over and pulled Rowan out of her saddle and onto his mount and grabbed her horse's reins.

Rowan was so focused on getting to the grove of trees that she was momentarily unaware of what was happening. When she realized that she was seated across the lap of a strange man, she opened her mouth and screamed. Then she began to struggle with all her might.

Max's mind was in a whirl. His blood was up! He had captured his prize! The blood of his Viking ancestors was roaring through his body and had completely taken over his brain. His arms were full of soft, fragrant female flesh that had been created just for him. Her scent was an intoxicating mix of flowers and spice. "Mine! Mine!" The word rang like a gong in his mind. Now all he had to do was find a private patch of wood and he could make her his forever!

These thoughts were somewhat disrupted by an object pounding on his chest. As Max's blood lust began to recede, he became aware that the woman he was holding in his arms was struggling against him. She was pounding on his chest with her fists and screaming at the top of her lungs. Miss Rowan was obviously not happy that he had saved her! But he was her hero, and he was even riding a white horse! Didn't she understand that he had saved her from possibly being shot by a sniper?

While this had been going on, Sheik had been slowing down, as had Miss Rowan's stallion. Max still had the stallion's reins in his hand. Sheik, sensing his rider's inattention, had slowed to a walk and had finally stopped.

As soon as the forward motion ceased, Rowan used all her might to break out of Max's grasp and slip to the ground.

She stalked angrily around in front of Sheik and pulled her stallion's reins from Max's grasp. Then, she marched to a place about ten feet behind her stallion, started to run and vaulted into her saddle as her brothers had taught her.

She adjusted her skirts and then turned to face Max. "What the great, perishing hell did you think you were doing?" she shouted at him. "Are you insane?"

He looked at her, truly puzzled. When Rowan saw his wide dark brown eyes staring into her own, she caught her breath. She had not realized, until that very moment, who the man was who had pulled her off her horse. "Him! Mine!" a voice shouted at the back of her mind.

"You!" she shouted.

To Max's ears, she didn't seem pleased to see him.

"You?" she said again, this time in a different tone. She sounded surprised and quite bemused.

It was at this point, when they were both staring at one another, that Rowan's party caught up with them.

"Who the damned devil do you think you are, abducting my sister like that?" shouted the gentleman who had been escorting the sisters. From his question, Max surmised that he was, indeed, one of the Higbee brothers.

"You dared to lay hands on her! You may have ruined her reputation beyond mending! I will have satisfaction!" he cried.

"Benedict! No!" exclaimed Rowan. "He was trying to save me! You can't call him out!"

"Benedict," thought Max. At least that answered that question. One of the prime breeders and trainers of horses in England. The one with the stables in Newmarket. Had the man just challenged him to a duel?

"I can't let strange men try to make off with you, Rowan, and not make an example of them!" her brother shouted.

"How dare he shout at his lovely Rowan?" Max thought.

"See here, Higbee," Max started to say.

"If you want to live to see another day, don't say another word, and stay where you are!" shouted Benedict at Max.

Max closed his mouth, just for a moment, he told himself, and sat still. Benedict was glowering alternately at his sister and at Max. Willow and Ivy now joined the discussion, if it could be called that.

"Benedict," said Willow urgently, "you forget that someone shot at us, or at least in our direction! We were all riding over to see if there were any clues left as to the identity of the shooter. Rowan was ahead of us!"

"It must have looked, to this gentlemen, like her horse was running away with her," said Ivy. There was quite a bit of force behind her rather mild words. "He acted as only a true gentleman should, pursing Rowan's runaway mount and saving her from severe injury!" She turned to Max and sighed. "He's a true hero! Can't you tell? He's even riding a white horse!"

"We've got to get her to stop reading those Minerva Press novels!" thought Willow. "She's getting worse and worse! By the time the season is over, she'll be lost to rational thought."

"Nevertheless," said Benedict in a somewhat agitated voice, though he was obviously beginning to perceive things somewhat differently, "he had his hands on her! In public!"

"How could he save her without his hands?" asked Ivy, the soul of logic.

"Why didn't he just grab the reins and slow down her mount?" asked Benedict.

"In the heat of the moment, he acted in what he thought was the best manner," explained Willow, in the voice of a sister who always has to explain things to brothers. "There was no time to consider alternatives! Really Benedict," she said. "What would you have done in the situation? If it was one of us?"

"To think that any one of my sisters would require that kind of help, is nothing short of ludicrous," said Benedict, indignantly. "You are all bruising riders. Everyone knows that," he said somewhat belligerently.

"On Edanmore, certainly," said Ivy. "But not here in town! No one knows us, really — despite all the silliness we've had to endure. "Why, we don't even know this gentleman," she continued." Think, Benedict! Step back from being the injured brother for a moment. This gentleman thought that he was doing a good deed! He thought that he was saving Rowan!"

There was silence for a moment. Grey, who had been listening to this conversation with interest, chose that minute to speak.

"I say, Mr. Higbee," he began quietly.

"And who the bloody hell are you?" was Benedict's belligerent response.

"Wellesly Glen," Grey responded politely, nodding his head, "at your service. And this gentleman, whose only fault in this matter was to attempt to save a young lady from injury, is…"

"Finally," thought Max. "The INTRODUCTION."

"Benedict," interrupted Willow. "Other people are coming! We can't be seen standing here like this with a man to whom we are not related, and to whom we have not been introduced! No one else saw what happened! Come! We must head back for home immediately if some ridiculous rumor is to be averted." With that, Willow turned her horse and began to gallop away, Ivy and the grooms following her.

"You haven't heard the end of this!" said Benedict in a menacing tone to Max. "Rowan!" he said curtly. "Come along! We've stayed here long enough!" With a nod to Grey, he followed his sisters. Rowan galloped up to join him without a backward glance at Max.

*"I had the thought that she didn't realize
that I was her hero ..."*

# CHAPTER NINE
## *Searching for Clues.*

*Gentlemen, among themselves, tend to use very bad
language given the slightest opportunity. Sometimes they use
impolite words without any provocation at all! If they are truly
gentlemen, they will never do so when ladies are present so as
to protect our tender sensibilities. And what of women? Should
a young lady use the slightest indelicate word, she is roundly
condemned. Why is that? Well may you ask! Here is the truth,
young ladies. Gentlemen recoil from women whose language
is less than pristine because they wonder where a lady could
have learned those words. To spare a gentleman's sensibilities,
a wise woman will restrict her use of rough language to those
occasions when she is with her peers. Make sure that the door
is closed and no one is listening at the keyhole! Remember
ladies, doors can have ears!*

*— Lady X's Admonitions to Young Women (Third Edition, 1802)*

"Really?" thought Max. "Again? I wasn't introduced again? And now she's giving me the cut direct? How are we ever going to have a dozen children if I can't manage an introduction to her?"

Max then said a number of very bad words. The Higbee party was out of earshot, which was just as well. Grey heard every word. He reflected that some of the words his friend had uttered were unknown to him. He wondered if Max had learned them in his service to the Crown as a spy. He'd have to ask Max about them when things had calmed down. Max turned to him.

"If I didn't know better," said Max, "I would say that some evil spirit is conspiring to keep me from my intended! You were just about to introduce me and Miss Willow interrupted! Couldn't she have waited just a minute more? Really Grey, this is beginning to be ridiculous! What do I have to do to get a proper introduction to my future countess?"

"Maybe Miss Willow felt that it was not the proper situation in which to introduce you to Miss Higbee," he replied. "After all, she knows her sister and the way she thinks."

Max sighed. Reluctantly he said, "You may be right. But it's still frustrating!"

"Let's go look in that grove of trees to see if we can come up with anything to tell us who the shooter was. You agree the shooting was intentional?" asked Grey.

"Absolutely. There's nothing to shoot at in the park. Hard to imagine a poacher trying to fill his family's pot here. Maybe you should be the spy," responded Max. "I'm certainly not doing a very good job of it these days."

"You're distracted," said Grey. "Love does that to a man. Once you and Miss Higbee are officially introduced, things will proceed very smoothly."

"At this point, I'd settle for just a little more smoothly," responded Max.

"Don't be such a pessimist," said Grey as the two men rode over to a thick grove of closely planted oak trees. They dismounted and spent the next few minutes looking for clues. Who would have wanted to shoot at the Higbee party? And why?

For Max, the "who" and the "why" were equally important. It wasn't clear to him which member of Rowan's party was the intended victim of the shooter. Some of the Season's new hopefuls or their mothers, might well have wanted to eliminate the three sisters. The Higbee sisters, thought Max, were getting much more than their fair share of attention in London's ballrooms.

Of course, it was unlikely that any one of those spurned young ladies would know how to shoot a rifle.

"Grey," said Max as they were both carefully looking through the grass for footprints or for anything that the shooter might have dropped, "what if he didn't really want to hit anyone?"

"You've got a point," said Grey. "There were so many people clustered together. The shooter, if he was any good at all, should have been able to hit someone! Or even, perish the thought, a horse. But despite the great number of targets, it seems that the bullet didn't even come close to grazing anyone. The villain could have been either a terrible shot or a really well-trained marksman."

"But why?" asked Max. "That question bothers me the most. Why shoot at the party if you didn't have an actual target?"

The two men continued to search the ground, slowly expanding their search.

"Look here!" shouted Max, pointing at a patch of soft earth about 10 feet away from the area where they had started. Grey hurried over to see what his friend had found.

"Hoofprints," said Max. "And look at the erosion on the bark of this young tree. A horse was tied up here. You can see where it trampled down the grass and where it was grazing. It must have been here for some time. It even left some evidence of its stay." He pointed to a small pile of manure.

All the evidence of the horse's presence is very fresh," said Max. I think we can deduce that the horse belonged to the shooter and was brought here in order to facilitate a quick retreat quickly once the deed was done.

"I agree," replied Grey.

Max was pacing around the small area in which the "evidence of horse" was located. He kept looking up in the direction in which the shot was fired.

"What was he up to?" asked Max, looking again at the hoof print. "It would be so helpful if there was an unusual nick on the horse's shoe that could lead us to the identity of the shooter.

"That only happens in novels or fairy stories," interjected Grey.

Max looked at the evidence and back again at the area in which the sisters and their entourage had clustered. "You might just have a point."

"A point?" asked Grey. "What point?"

"Novels and fairy stories," said Max. "After I had pulled Rowan from her horse, she was very angry. She was beating my chest with her fists. She's got quite a punch!" he said, chuckling. "When we're married, I'm going to have to watch my step! I guess that comes from her having eight brothers."

"What point?" prodded Grey.

"Well," continued Max, "she was struggling to get away. I had the thought that she didn't realize that I was her hero even though I was riding a white horse! Like in a fairy tale! The men of the ton are besotted with the Flame Sisters, as the gossip sheets call them. It is almost impossible to get to meet them — as I know all too well. What if one of these men was so desperate to meet one of them that he decided to create a situation in which the young ladies were seemingly in danger? Then he rides to the rescue and saves them."

"If what you're saying is true, then the poor devil must have had a real shock when the sisters turned and rode toward him! And to make things worse, you interfered to play the hero and made off with Miss Higbee!" said Grey. "I think you've got the right of it," he continued. "Can you imagine the poor fool's frustration when his plan went so horribly awry? I almost feel sorry for him!"

"Indeed," replied Max. "But what really concerns me is, if the fellow is so unhinged that he thought that shooting at the girls was a good way to get their attention, what will he try next?"

"That is troubling," agreed Grey.

"The Higbee family needs to know that the sisters may be in danger," said Max. "But who would be the best person to tell them? If I attempt to call on Benedict, I'm afraid he'll call me out before I can speak my piece."

"I'm sure that the sisters will have calmed him down by now," replied Grey. "They are certainly intrepid young ladies! When they turned, almost as one, and started racing toward that grove of trees, I was absolutely dumbstruck! I've never seen anything as wonderful or as terrifying in my life! What if the shooter had wanted to take another shot? What if he was really aiming at one or all of them?

"I tell you, Max, can you imagine being their brother?" continued Grey. "No wonder Benedict was so upset! One of them would be enough to drive a man insane, but the three of them together? Are you sure that you want to take on Miss Higbee? She's the worst of the lot! The way she raced toward the trees on that bay stallion was nothing short of thrilling. She rides like her brother, completely at one with the horse. She'd make a marvelous jockey, although she's a little too tall for the job."

"She's not too tall at all," responded Max. "She's just the right height." Then he frowned, wondering what the hell he was talking about. The memory of holding Rowan in his arms came racing back and almost felled him. She was just the right height for all sorts of things!

Grey laughed as though he knew just what his friend was talking about.

"What a mess, Grey," said Max. "What are we going to do?

"Have we seen everything there is to be seen here?" asked Grey.

"Barring some deluded lunatic coming by and confessing" responded Max, "I don't think we're going to learn anything more here today. We're looking for a besotted idiot who would like to become a hero for any one of the famous Flame Sisters and make her his forever heroine.

"You're right," said Grey. "We need to figure out a plan to keep the Higbee sisters safe from the lovesick lunatic who wants to hunt them down."

"The Lovesick Lunatic. That's a good title for a chilling story, don't you think, Grey? Perhaps if I don't manage to secure my bride, I will lock myself in a tower somewhere and write it."

Despite his concern for his friend and for the Higbee sisters, Grey laughed.

"You always told the best stories late at night when we were at Cambridge. You'd probably be good at it," he said.

"Come back with me for breakfast. I think some sustenance is in order," said Max. "We can strategize over strong cups of coffee."

An hour later, the two friends sat at Max's breakfast table finishing off a meal of kippers, eggs, muffins and marmalade. Max had just requested another pot of coffee. He and Grey needed fuel.

"The Higbee sisters are really in danger. They need more protection when they go out," Max said. "Do you think we can trust Benedict to convey the seriousness of the situation to his father?"

"I doubt that he saw the situation the same way we did," said Grey. "He seemed more upset by you having your hands all over his sister Rowan than on the attack itself. You, or we, may need to call on the baron and tell him of our concerns."

"Speaking with the baron and Benedict together would probably be a good idea," said Max. "If I show up alone, Benedict may have the wrong handle on things."

Grey laughed. "Ironic, isn't it? You would like nothing more than to call on the baron and ask for Miss Higbee's hand in marriage. You've had her in your arms, her brother wants to duel with you over her honor, and you haven't yet been properly introduced! What a coil! Is it being a spy that contributes to this roundaboutation?"

"It's certainly odd, isn't it?" replied Max. "This whole situation makes me feel as if there is some outside force moving things around just to make my life more difficult! If I were actually on a case, I would believe that there was some mastermind plotting in the background. But really, the whole thing is, or was, very simple until today. Go to a ball, see the woman I know I must marry, get an introduction, convince her to love me, propose, get married and live happily ever after. What could be more straightforward than that? Yet nothing about this has been simple."

"And now we have to call upon her father and tell him that some lunatic may be stalking his daughters in order to meet them," said Grey.

"Do you think that I could ask him to introduce me to Rowan while we're at the house?" asked Max.

"How would that go exactly?" asked Grey. "Would you please introduce me to your daughter Rowan, my lord? Although I had her in my arms today, we have never formally met and I would like her to be my wife."

"I guess that's a 'no,'" said Max glumly.

"Let's see what happens," said Grey. "Perhaps there will be an opportunity that can be exploited.

"I'll write a note to the baron asking for a meeting as soon as possible," said Max. "He needs to know the entirety of the situation so he can decide on a course of action to keep the girls safe. I'm attached to the military. Do you think that he might consider making me Rowan's personal protector?"

"One thing at a time, my friend," replied Grey. "Go write your note and send it off with your swiftest footman."

Max pushed back his chair, stood up and walked toward the door of the breakfast room.

He stopped when he heard Grey call to him.

"Max," he said, "keep the note short and to the point. Make sure that you don't add a postscript asking for Rowan's hand in marriage!"

Max stepped back to the table, grabbed an orange out of a bowl on the sideboard, and threw it at Grey. It hit his friend square in the chest.

"Very mature, Max," laughed Grey. "Just what I'd expect from a master spy in the Admiralty's employ!"

Grey's laughter followed Max all the way to his study.

*"I just don't see any other way out ..."*

# CHAPTER TEN
## *A Bad Plan Gets Worse!*

*All's fair in love and war. Plotting to get what you want, young ladies, is all well and good. A successful undertaking requires careful planning and perfect execution. Reconnaissance — and the examination of every detail — is crucial. Know your opponent! Know his likes and dislikes, his habits, his haunts. The better your information, the greater the possibility of your success! Knowledge is power, young ladies! Knowledge is power!*

—*Lady X's Admonitions to Young Women (Third Edition, 1802)*

Flavia St John paced around her threadbare bedroom in her family's seemingly prosperous Mayfair home. She was running her fingers nervously through her brown curls. Her bright hazel eyes were dimmed with anxiety.

She stared at herself in the small mirror that hung on the back of the door to her room. In the dim light, her prominent sharp nose looked particularly angular. She was waiting for her younger twin brother, Frederick, Baron Hilton, to return from his urgent morning mission. If he wasn't successful, their entire family would be in serious trouble.

Flavia had just come in from sweeping the outside stairs and walkway and had washed her hands in the cold water in the basin next to her bed. For the last two years, ever since most of her family's household staff had been dismissed, she had made it a practice to wake up every morning before daylight and perform the task of sweeping the stairs and walkway herself. At that hour of the morning, no one would see her doing a servant's work.

It was important that the house look well-kept from the outside. If people knew how desperate her family was for funds, both Flavia's and her twin's futures would be ruined. It astounded Flavia that her parents did not seem to grasp this simple fact of ton life. And why didn't they question how the front entrance to their home was so well kept? She acknowledged that perhaps they were just too self-absorbed to consider the practical aspects of life. At times, she wondered if her parents believed in elves or fairies.

As Flavia awaited her brother's return, she thought about how her family had come to these desperate straits. She had been aware, ever since her 13th birthday, that her parents' consciousness of the realities of life — things like having enough money to buy food and coal and pay the cook — was sadly lacking. To celebrate her birthday, her mother had invited six of Flavia's young female cousins and their

mothers to an afternoon tea. All of the sandwiches
and pastries had been ordered from Fortnum & Mason,
the famous emporium on Piccadilly. The family no longer
employed a pastry cook.

Flavia had a new dress for the occasion, even though it
was a hand-me-down from a cousin who had outgrown it.
Her mother, still a beauty, though her fine brown hair was
beginning to thin and go grey, was wearing her best day
dress. It was several seasons out of fashion, but it had been
freshened up with some new ribbon trim.

Flavia's twin, Frederick, younger than his sister by
fifteen minutes, had been taken to Hyde Park to fly a new
kite his father had given him for his birthday. Spending time
with his often-distracted father was a treat for him.

As Flavia's guests were leaving, a loud knocking on the
door was heard. Herald, their man of all work, answered the
door. A minute later, Flavia heard raised voices and the sound
of scuffling. Her mother went to the door of the parlor and
looked out toward the entry way. What she saw made her go
pale. The fine lines around her mouth deepened with anxiety.
She turned to the guests and, instead of ushering them to the
front door, she whispered, "Come with me, ladies! We're
going to play a game!"

Flavia's mother went to a picture hanging on a side
wall. She pressed the corner of the frame, and the wall slid
partially to one side, revealing an opening.

"Come with me! We're going to leave the house
through our secret passage," she said urgently, as the
sound of footsteps and men shoving one another came closer
to the parlor.

Flavia, her cousins and their mothers were all hurried into the passage. Her mother pushed a small button and the wall went back into its place, only now everyone was on the other side. Her mother encouraged the group to move forward. She led them down winding steps and through twisting halls to a door that opened outward into the mews. Her guests out and looked about themselves, puzzled.

"Wasn't that fun?" asked Flavia's mother in a somewhat forced gay tone. "Come," she said. "I will lead you out to the street so that you can find your carriages."

"Mother," said one of Flavia's young cousins, "I don't have my new hat and gloves!"

"Oh, don't worry about that," responded Flavia's mother. "I'll have our footman return your garments later today. The noise you heard were some workmen come to do repairs on the house. They were bringing in dusty equipment to do their work, and I didn't want your garments to be soiled."

They had reached the street.

"Thank you all for coming to our birthday fête for our dear Flavia," said her mother. "We must do this again next year!"

Flavia and her mother returned to the house by the kitchen door. As they were about to enter, they heard Flavia's father's voice raised in anger. "They must have returned from the park," thought Flavia.

"Go up to your room, lock the door, and stay there," said her mother sharply. "Do not come out until I come for you. Do as I say! Right away!" She gave Flavia a push toward the servants' stairs that led to the family wing.

Flavia was puzzled and a little frightened by her mother's tone, but she was an obedient girl and hurried up the servants' steps to her room. As soon as she had locked her door and pushed a chair under the door handle for good measure — a heroine had done that to stay safe in a novel she had read — she hurried to her window and looked out onto the street.

There was a large cart pulled up in front of the house. Two burly men were coming out of the front door carrying what seemed to be all the furniture from the front parlor. As Flavia watched, they filled the cart. A third man came out of the house carrying what looked like the new damask drapes from the parlor in his arms. He placed the drapes over the furniture and pulled a large piece of cloth over the entire contents. Then, he climbed up into the cart and it pulled away from the house.

Flavia was frozen in place. What was happening?

There was a knock on her door. She hurried across the room, removed the chair, unlocked the door and opened it. Her brother was standing there with a confused look on his face. Flavia reached out and pulled him into her bedroom, shutting and locking the door behind him.

"Did you see what was happening?" Flavia asked him before he could utter a word.

"What's going on?" asked Frederick.

"I don't know," responded his sister. "One moment, we were saying goodbye to our guests, and the next thing I knew, mother was dragging us through a secret doorway. We came out into the mews. Then she told me to come up to my room and lock myself in. I've been watching men taking away our parlor furnishings."

"Why would they want our furniture?" he asked. "What could they possibly do with it?"

Flavia thought for a minute, pacing back and forth.

"It's not all that new, but it was expensive when it was first purchased," she responded. "I guess it could be sold. You know that mother and father have been having some problems with money in the last year. Maybe they have a creditor that arranged to take the furniture and sell it to settle their bill."

"Tradesmen don't do that to aristocrats!" said Frederick haughtily. "They wait to be paid."

Flavia nodded her head in agreement. She knew that was generally the case, but Flavia knew something about her parents that her twin didn't know.

"I overheard father complain to mother that the crops at our estate last year had been bad, and that the tenants were lazy. I also think mother and father have been gambling very heavily over the past year to make up for those losses. Maybe there's a connection.

Frederick nodded his head.

"It's possible, I guess," he said.

There was a sharp knock on the door. A voice called out Flavia's name. It was their mother.

Flavia unlocked the door and her mother entered the room.

Flavia didn't give her mother a chance to say anything. "Mother," she said, "what is going on? Why did those men take away our furniture and the new drapes? Why did you tell our guests that they were workmen come to do repairs?"

Her mother looked at Flavia. Then she noticed her son looking out the window.

"Frederick," she said, "go play cards with your father. Flavia and I need to have a talk."

He looked at his mother and then at Flavia. She gave a slight nod of her head. Her brother always looked to Flavia for direction and followed her lead. He made a slight bow to his mother and left the room.

"Sit down, Flavia," said her mother. "I have something serious to tell you."

"Now that you're 13, you need to begin to see the world through the eyes of an adult. Do you understand?"

Flavia said, "Yes, mother," even though she had no idea what her mother meant.

"Your father," her mother continued, "is the love of my life, but he is a very poor manager. To put it plainly, we have very little money. Our ancestral estate in Sussex has never been particularly prosperous, and your father has always liked to gamble. Unfortunately, he is not a lucky gambler. He loses more money than he wins.

"I'm telling you this because it directly affects your future. Now that you are 13, you are nearing the age when you can make an advantageous marriage. When you are 17, we will give you a Season. It will be your job to find and marry a man of wealth and position by the end of that Season. Failure is not an option. If you don't marry by the end of your Season, you may have to become a companion to an elderly woman. We won't have the funds to support you.

"Your brother will inherit this house, the seat in Sussex and any money that is left. He will, of course, marry an heiress of appropriate lineage. You can't expect that he will be willing to have you live with him. It is his job to marry and beget at least an heir and a spare, so that our family line can continue. His wife, who will bring her money to the marriage, may not be willing to support her husband's spinster sister. Then you will have to go into service."

Flavia was stunned. She didn't know what to say. She was filled with a sense of soul-deadening despair. How could one's life change so dramatically in just a few hours? This morning, she had awoken with a sense of excitement about her birthday tea party and her grown-up dress. The party had been lovely, the food delicious. Then the creditors had arrived, and her mother had explained Flavia's future. She had four years to become everything that some man, any man, would want in a wife.

Sitting in her room, listening to her mother, Flavia made a vow. She would dedicate herself to keeping the family ship financially afloat. She would find ways to save money and set some of it aside for her own needs. She would not permit her parents to rob her of a happy future. She would work hard to become that a perfect young lady so that she could marry by the end of her one Season.

From that day on, Flavia paid very close attention to her parents' actions. She found out where they kept their money and how they handled their bills and the servants' wages. When she thought that they had been gambling, she would wait until they were asleep. Then, she would sneak into their sitting room and count the money they had deposited in a box they kept in a special drawer in a side table.

Flavia maintained an accounting of the money in that box. She had a governess when she was younger and had excelled in mathematics. The years she turned 10, the governess left and was not replaced. By that time, Flavia had learned the fundamentals of keeping household accounts. That skill proved to be very useful.

When Flavia checked the box, if there was less money than there had been before, she took one shilling and set it aside for herself. If there was more money, she would take half of the additional amount plus two shillings for herself. Her parents never seemed to notice that the amount of money in the bag varied.

The funds that Flavia kept for herself were stored in the belly of a cloth horse that her old nanny had made for her when she was a very little girl. Flavia slept with the horse next to her every night.

The funds for household expenses were stored in a locked box at the bottom of her wardrobe. She used that money to pay the servants when her parents had neglected to do so, or to give something to the butcher or the grocer when the household bill became too high and they refused to extend more credit. Her parents were oblivious to her machinations.

As she got older, Flavia worried that her parents would insist that she marry as soon as she turned 17. She knew of young girls who were married off to old, rich men to save their families. She feared her parents had decided marriage to an old, rich man was to be her destiny. Flavia determined this would not be her fate. She increased the amount of money she appropriated for her own use to four shillings and set aside less money for the household. When the time came, Flavia would be able to take care of herself.

Flavia's fears for her future were never far from her mind. She never had a Season. Her parents didn't explain this lapse, but she didn't need to ask. She knew it was because there was no money for even the most basic expenses, and she did not have a dowry. Flavia was fairly certain she had a long life as a spinster ahead of her.

In the last few months, their situation had seemed to deteriorate drastically. Her parents had begun selling everything of value in the house. The large, ornately framed paintings that had been collected by generations of Viscounts Somersby, were long gone to pay both parents' gambling debts. Over the years, Flavia had worked hard to save the family silver and the precious Persian rugs. Then, one morning, she woke up to find that they were all gone! Every time there was a knock at the door, Flavia expected it to be a creditor come to throw them all out onto the street.

Of course, they could always retreat to the family estate in Sussex, which was entailed and therefore couldn't be sold. The house hadn't been lived in for more than 20 years, and most likely needed extensive repairs. Living there would be extremely uncomfortable.

Flavia heard the front door open and close. It must be Frederick. Her parents didn't rise until the late morning. Without a butler, their three remaining servants, a cook, her mother's lady's maid and an elderly man of all work, were slow to rise in the morning.

Waiting for her brother to come up to her room, Flavia hoped that for once in his incompetent life, her twin had done something right!

She sensed, rather than heard, the door of her room creak open. Flavia turned to see her brother walk into the room and quietly close the door behind him. His shoulders were hunched forward and he hung his head.

"Oh damn," she thought in despair, "something has gone very badly awry."

Flavia walked toward Frederick and extended her hands to his, leading him to a chair in front of the unlit fireplace. They hadn't had fires in the bedrooms since mid-January. That was when their father had told them there was no money to supplement their dwindling store of coal.

"Tell me what happened," she said softly to her brother.

Frederick looked at her, his curly brown hair a windblown mess, his hazel eyes, so like hers, filled with remorse. His lips moved, but no sound came out. He took a deep breath and then began to speak.

"Our plan was so simple," he began. "There was no way for it to fail. All I had to do was perform some brave act in order to attract the attention of the Flame Sisters. Having met them, I would attract one of them and, after a brief courtship, marry her. Her dowry and her family's money would set our family to rights. It was a perfect plan. You are a brilliant strategist," he said, looking at his sister with a weak smile.

"The idea of creating a seemingly dangerous situation when the Flame Sisters were riding in the park, and then coming to their rescue, was genius. It should have worked perfectly. I was to go to a stand of trees and wait for them. Then, when I saw them, I was to shoot towards them and then ride to their rescue," Frederick continued.

"I did it just as we planned, even to hiring a white horse from the stables. I got to the trees early and settled down to wait. I had practiced with the rifle so that I would be sure not to hit anyone. Finally, I saw the sisters and their escorts. The boot boy from Edanmore House was correct in his information that they would ride out early today if the weather was fair."

"So, you were all set to shoot and then ride to their rescue," said Flavia. "What happened? Oh goodness," she exclaimed. "You didn't hit anyone, did you?"

"No. No! Not at all," her twin hurried to reassure her. "Nothing like that. It was the damnedest thing. When I got off the shot, I expected at least one of them to shout, or faint or something! I was already untying to horse so that I could ride to their rescue. Instead of being alarmed and afraid, they all turned toward where I had been hiding, and came riding hell bent toward the trees! Well, what could I do? There was no way to ride up behind them. I jumped on the horse and rode away as quickly as I could!"

"Oh Frederick! Of all the awful luck!" cried his sister. "They're probably the only young women in the world who would try to hunt down a villain by themselves! If only they had been like most ladies of the ton! They would have dithered, cried and fainted as I had expected. Oh! What are we going to do? How are we going to stay out of that crumbling ruin of a house in Sussex?"

Frederick jumped out of the chair and then sat down again. He began tearing at his hair and muttering "What to do? What to do?" His eyes examined every item in the room as it came into his line of vision.

He saw a piece of paper on the floor and went to pick it up. It was a newssheet that Flavia had been reading. He asked his sister, "What is this?

She grimaced. "It's a copy of *The Ton Reporter*," she replied. "I was reading all about the latest doings of the fabulous Flame Sisters before I went to sleep last night."

Frederick looked down at the paper, a slight frown on his face. Flavia looked at him quizzically.

"You're getting an idea," she said.

"Do you keep these?" asked Frederick.

"What? *The Ton Reporter?*" asked Flavia.

"Yes, *The Ton Reporter.*"

"I've been saving them for kindling," said Flavia, "but mother hasn't let me light a fire for weeks. There's a stack over there in the corner." She pointed to some papers near the fireplace. "Why do you want them?"

"I read something. I think it was early in the Season, but it's giving me an idea. I'd like to read the article again. Help me bring the papers over here and arrange them in date order. Then I'll go through them one at a time."

There weren't that many issues to organize and soon Frederick was settled in a chair, scanning the articles one by one. After about fifteen minutes, he cried, "I've found it. Listen to this!"

He began to read aloud.

*The rash of kidnappings of heiresses during the Little Season in the fall, is having interesting results. The marriage of Lady P— to her fortune-hunting kidnapper, Lord C— seems to be a happy one. The couple are in expectation of a blessed event....The marriage of Lady G — and her kidnapper, Baron S — will take place next week at St. George's Church... after the race to Gretna Green, Lady G — 's parents bowed to the inevitable. Parents! Watch your daughters carefully!*

Frederick had a big smile on his face.

"Well, what do you think?" he asked Flavia.

"What do I think about what?" she replied.

"Kidnapping one of the sisters, of course," he answered. "It's a perfect plan! Once the sister has been away overnight, her family will have to let me marry her!"

"That's crazy! And dangerous," said Flavia. "And what happens if you get caught before you manage to keep the sister away overnight? They might hang you, Frederick! No! It's much too dangerous. Things are bad enough! I can't lose you!"

"No! You don't understand," said her brother. "I won't do it myself. I'll hire some people to do it. Then I'll find the sister for the family, and they'll be grateful to me and agree to let me court their daughter. She'll marry me to save her reputation."

Flavia sat quietly for a minute, thinking. Frederick's plan was unclear. Depending on her brother was rarely a good idea, although he always meant well, but what could they do? The creditors were at the door.

Taking a deep breath she said, "Do you really think it will work? Look what happened this morning. Those girls are totally unpredictable. Who knows what they'll do? Besides, who would you kidnap?"

"Ivy, the youngest one," said Frederick. "Or maybe I should have her and the middle sister, Willow, kidnapped at the same time. Then I'd have a greater chance of getting one of them to marry me."

"I don't know, Frederick," said Flavia. "What about their oldest sister, Rowan?"

"She's too old for me," said Frederick, "and besides, she scares me to death. You should have seen the way she set out to see who had shot at them! She looked like an Amazon warrior female on that horse. Leave her out of it!"

Flavia laughed weakly. "Alright," she said, "your plan might work, but how would you even get your hired men close to the girls? They are always chaperoned."

Frederick sighed. "You're right. It was a good idea, but getting close to them might be very difficult."

"If we knew their social schedule..." said Flavia. "I'm sure they attend all the most fashionable events."

"There must be a way," said Frederick.

Flavia frowned and then her face cleared, and she smiled.

"Mama got an invitation from Aunt Fontaine last week," she said. "Aunt Fontaine is hosting a Venetian Breakfast at the house in Richmond. It's coming up fairly soon. Mama turned it down of course. We don't have the clothing to wear to an event like that, but it was nice of aunt to send us the invitation. I'm sure that the Flame Sisters and their family were invited and will attend."

"A party in the country might make it easier to spirit the sisters away without anyone noticing for a while," said Frederick. "They have that big maze near the back of the property. There's a secret exit near the center. Remember when we got lost one summer when we were visiting? Cousin Gerard found us and led us out that way."

"Maybe cousin Gerard could be convinced to help us. He's always been kind of sweet on you, Flavia. Perhaps if you asked him, told him at least part of the truth, he'd be willing to help."

Flavia looked thoughtful. She was concerned about this plan. It seemed dangerous to her. Was it possible that Frederick could come up with a practical plan? She began to wonder aloud if this scheme could work.

"Perhaps if we told Gerard it was a prank," Flavia mused, "he might be persuaded to encourage the girls to explore the maze. Frederick, do you really think you could find some men who would be willing to do this?"

"I have some friends who are always up for a lark," he said, "especially if there's some blunt involved."

"It always comes down to money," said Flavia.

"Whoever I hired would want something," said Frederick. "But I think these friends might be bought off cheaply. They would think this was just a big joke. Having it involve the Flame Sisters would give them incentive. I don't think they've met them yet."

"How would you get the money?" asked Flavia. She very deliberately suppressed her knowledge of her savings.

Frederick frowned, took a deep breath and said, "I still have the gold buttons from my favorite waistcoat. When things began to look very bad, I took them off and replaced them with brass. I've been holding them back in case of an emergency. I can sell them for enough to pay off my friends for their cooperation and even have a little left over to set aside."

Flavia threw herself at her brother and hugged him. She never thought that he could be so practical.

"I'm not sure this will work. Let me get my journal, and we'll write down every detail of the plan. We can't afford to have this fail. If this is going to take place at the Venetian Breakfast, we don't have much time."

"I'm sure that once you have the plan all written out, you'll see that it can work," said Frederick. "And you will certainly be able to convince Gerard to help us."

"This has to work or it's the rest of all of our lives in a crumbling pile in Sussex," said Flavia.

"This is a very dangerous undertaking, but I just don't see any other way out ... "

*"If Max didn't know better, he would have
thought that they were all together to take tea."*

# CHAPTER ELEVEN
## An Alliance Is Formed.

*Men, young ladies, are among the silliest of God's*
*creatures. They are ruled not by their rational minds, as are*
*women, but by their little heads. Does this shock you, my*
*dears? There are some things that you must know in order to*
*prevail in the age-old battle between women and men.*
*When a man becomes jealous, it is not because he has a*
*rational reason to do so. Never approach a man with reason!*
*Men do not understand that women are the reasoning*
*sex. Instead, appeal to his desires. You will be much more*
*successful in getting what you want and need.*

*—Lady X's Admonitions to Young Women (Third Edition, 1802)*

Max's note to Baron Edanmore was answered promptly. At
one o'clock later that day, Max and Grey presented their cards
at the door of Edanmore House and were shown into the baron's

study. The baron was seated behind a large desk that faced away from the interior of the room. When seated at it, he gazed out on a magnificent rose garden that was just beginning to bloom. He turned to greet his visitors, gave a slight nod when they entered, and motioned for them to be seated on well-padded chairs grouped in a circle at the side of the room.

As the young men walked toward the seating area, they realized that they were not alone with the baron. There were several people already seated in a circle. The lovely older woman, thought Max, was most likely the baron's wife. Benedict, the son that they had met that morning, sat next to the baroness looking somewhat belligerent. A slightly younger version of the baron sat next to his father. Also present were the three Flame sisters. Everyone rose in greeting as Max and Grey walked toward the empty chairs that were waiting for them.

Lady Edanmore motioned for the visitors to be seated. If Max didn't know better, he would have thought that they were all together to take tea. The baron spoke.

"Benedict and my daughters told me of the incident in the park," he began without a preamble. Turning to Max he asked, "Have you come to ask for Rowan's hand in marriage? If so, I must tell you that such a gesture is not necessary. I do not believe that your actions in the park, as described by my son and my daughters, constitutes anything improper. If there is any talk, we will deal with it."

Before Max could say a word, Rowan jumped out of her chair.

"Father," she said, "I have not even been introduced to this gentleman!" she exclaimed. "Why would he offer marriage? I told you that Benedict's description of events was positively medieval!" She sat down in her chair with an exaggerated flounce and crossed her arms over her chest.

The son who had not been introduced stood, turned to Max and walked over to him, his hand outstretched.

"Blake Higbee, Foreign Office," he said as he and Max shook hands. "It's very good to meet you at last, Lord Darby. I've heard about your impressive work with the Admiralty. Please permit me to formally introduce my parents, Baron and Baroness Edanmore, one of my younger brothers, Mr. Benedict Higbee, co-founder and proprietor of Edanmore Stud in Newmarket, and my lovely sisters, who, in case you've been dwelling in a cave these past few weeks, are in London to make their bows to society, "Miss Rowan Higbee and the Misses Willow and Ivy."

"Finally," thought Max. "The ice is broken!"

"Finally," thought Grey, "he can get on with his wooing."

Max bowed formally to each of the members of the family as they were introduced. Then he said, "May I make known to you my most trusted friend, Lord Richard Grey Birmingham, the Earl of Wellesly Glen. We have been close friends since our first day at Cambridge. He was with me this morning."

Grey bowed in acknowledgement of this introduction.

"He's with the Admiralty," thought Rowan. "He doesn't have a title like 'captain.' Does that mean he works on land? What does someone who works for the Admiralty and doesn't go to sea actually do?" she wondered. "Blake knows about him. He mentioned Lord Darby's work." She mused about this for a moment. Then she thought, "I wonder if he's a spy?" She found this thought very exciting and compelling.

As Rowan was musing about Max, he had begun to address the baron once again.

"I take it that some version of the events of this morning have been made known to you," he said. The baron nodded. Max continued. "The presence of your son from the Foreign Office suggests that you were given a fairly accurate account of the incident, and that you recognize that there is a threat to your daughters.

"The earl and I asked for a meeting with you to advise you of other information that we were able to gather once your daughters and their party headed toward safety," Max continued. "We took quite a bit of time examining the area where the shooter hid. From the evidence we found there, we have deduced that there was a single gunman, presumably acting alone, who arrived and left on horseback."

"It is not clear what motivated this attack," said Grey. "It seems pointless. But one thing is clear. Your daughters need to be better protected."

"There is another danger of which you should be aware," said Max. "This fall there was a rash of kidnapping of young heiresses. Although information has been circulating that your daughters have modest dowries, a fortune hunter might think it worthwhile to kidnap one of them and hold her for ransom. Your family worth, after all, is anything but modest. Thus far, no one has made such an attempt, but I strongly suggest that when the young ladies appear in public, there should be a stronger presence of armed retainers."

"I agree with your conclusions," said Blake. Turning toward his parents he continued.

"Lord Darby's work for the Admiralty makes him

particularly well suited for understanding the nuances of personal security. His assistance with developing ways to keep the girls safe could be invaluable. I suggest that Lord Darby and Lord Grey, perhaps with some minor support from my office, recruit a company of people to help guard our girls when they leave the house."

"I would be honored to help in any way that I can," said Max.

"You?" shouted Benedict, jumping to his feet and staring angrily at Max. "You accosted my sister this morning! Who's to protect her from you?"

"Benedict! Sit down!" said his stepmother. "You are being ridiculous! Lord Darby thought that he was saving Rowan! Far from being a rogue, he has shown that he is a truly honorable gentleman! I think that having him and Lord Birmingham escort the girls along with some of our people is a brilliant idea. What do you think, my love?" the baroness asked, turning to her husband.

"We're to escort the girls?" thought Max. "When was that suggestion made? Although, it's a wonderful idea!"

Baron Edanmore hadn't been married to his dear Rose Elizabeth for almost 25 years without learning to recognize the gleam of matchmaking in her twinkling blue eyes. Therefore, when prompted, he played his part to perfection.

"I'm not so sure, my dear," he said, frowning. "Lord Darby acted very precipitously. True, he believed that the girls, and Rowan in particular, were in danger. On the other hand, pulling her off her mount could have been dangerous for both our daughter and the animal. Perhaps we should do as Blake has suggested and recruit some people from the Home Office.

Or perhaps we could hire some Bow Street Runners to protect the girls. After all, they are trained for such things."

The baroness frowned. "But they are not gentlemen, my lord. How would it look for the girls to be surrounded by men of that sort? We wouldn't want to create the wrong sort of notice!"

"Too late for that," muttered Benedict. His stepmother shot him a quelling glance. Benedict obviously didn't understand that he had no lines in this particular scene. She continued.

"Lord Darby and Lord Birmingham are upstanding men of the ton! If anyone should comment on their constant presence in the girls' company, it would only be to suggest that perhaps they have caught the attention of one or more of our daughters."

At this statement, Max couldn't help smiling. The baroness had hit the nail right on the head! Good woman! Grey gulped and turned slightly pale. This was an unexpected turn of events! He liked Miss Willow and Miss Ivy, but only as he liked many young women. He was not ready to step into the parson's mousetrap and it looked like this plan was ideally suited to help that situation along.

The baron turned to his daughters.

"You girls will be most affected by the steps we take," the baron said. "Ivy, are you willing to be escorted by Lords Darby and Birmingham with some guards dressed as footman trailing behind when you go out?"

"I really think it is much ado about nothing, father," said Ivy. "It was only the one time, and I'm sure it was just a poor, love-sick young man who perpetrated this evil deed. Surely, he has decided to mend his ways. Can't we go on as before?"

"I love you as a father," the baron said, "but I cannot be quite so cavalier as to believe that this will all go away."

"You *are* my father," said Ivy, smiling at their joke.

"Willow, what do you think?" the baron asked.

Willow glanced at Rowan and then said, "I agree with Ivy, but I also agree with you, father. There would be no harm in having some extra protection when we go out. Having Lords Darby and Birmingham as escorts would be acceptable. I've only danced with Lord Birmingham once, but he seemed a pleasant young man. If Lord Darby is his closest friend, I'm sure that he must also be an amiable gentleman. And Lord Darby was very dashing this morning," she concluded, smiling slightly at Rowan. "I say yes to the scheme of having their escort for a time until we know that the villain who shot at us is captured or at least warned off."

"Benedict," said the baron, "I believe that I know your feelings, but please feel free to have your say."

"I say no!" said Benedict, jumping to his feet again and beginning to pace. "I don't like the way Darby looks at Rowan. It's as if she's a ripe piece of fruit that he just has to sample!"

"Don't be vulgar, Benedict," said the baroness in an aside. Undaunted, Benedict continued.

"I think Darby is up to no good where Rowan is concerned, although I would trust him with Willow and Ivy. Let's call in a few of the brothers and set up a rotation for escorting the girls. Let's keep it in the family!" Having reached his chair once again, Benedict sat down in such a way that it was clear he was making a statement.

"Benedict dear," said the baroness, exasperated, but with a smile. She really had some work to do with this son. He was missing the nuances of the situation. The problem was that Benedict hadn't spent enough time with the family lately. She would have to take him in hand before she could pass him on to a nice young woman for training. She sighed and continued.

"Your brothers are all married and have duties to their wives, their children and their professions. Even Blake, although I'm sure he'd make time if we asked, must put his duty to king and country first. We can't demand that your brothers become escorts for their sisters for the entire season. You're the only one who is not married and has the time for such things."

"There," thought Rose. "Let him chew on that!"

"A brilliant summation my dear, but nothing less than what I would expect from you," said the baron. He turned to Max and Grey. "Is this arrangement agreeable to you both? If not, I would certainly understand. We are asking for a great deal of your time. The girls have an extremely active social schedule. Do you each have time to undertake this mission for the next month or so?

"It would be an honor, my lord, to serve as protector and defender to your lovely daughters for as long as needs be," replied Max, smiling.

"I also, am willing and able to put myself in the service of your family," responded Grey rather formally. "At the present time, I do not vote my seat in the Lords, so my time is my own."

At that statement, Ivy's head shot up and she looked at Grey with narrowed eyes, but she said nothing.

"Excellent," said the baron. "It's decided then." Looking at his wife and daughters he continued. "We shall form an escort for the girls composed of Benedict, Lord Darby and

Lord Birmingham and supported by some of our most able footmen. There are several who have served in the military. It's the perfect solution. Benedict can guarantee that the other gentleman are scrupulously correct in their behavior toward the girls, as I know they will be. And Benedict's concern for his sisters' safety will be appeased because he will always be on hand to protect them."

At this statement, Benedict sputtered, but said nothing. The baron continued.

"Perhaps when the fellow who staged that scene this morning sees the girls in the company of three such outstanding gentlemen, he will just give up and fix his attentions elsewhere."

Turning toward Max and Grey, the baron asked, "Perhaps you gentlemen would stay after this meeting and review the girls' calendar with their mother.

"We would be pleased to do so, my lord," said Max. "And after a month or so, we should have a feeling about whether the villain has moved on or not."

"A month!" said Benedict! "I can't stay in town a month! I've important work to see to in Newmarket! I thought only to stay a week or two in London, at the most!"

"But Benedict dear," said his stepmother, "this was all your idea! Surely you don't intend to leave the complete care and protection of your sisters to these seemingly very nice gentlemen whom we barely know? I'm sure they would do very well, but they're not family."

Benedict groaned and ran his fingers through his already somewhat disheveled auburn hair. "Mother," he said in a voice that was pleading. That was all he said.

"It's up to you, my dear," she replied. "I would never dictate to any of my boys. If you can't be here, perhaps Lord Darby has a friend who could fill in as the third escort. After all, each of the girls will need a person to watch out for her security."

Turning to Max, the baroness said, "Lord Darby, is there a gentleman of your acquaintance, perhaps someone with whom you work at the Admiralty, who could be a substitute for Benedict?"

Before Max could reply, Benedict interrupted.

"Lord Darby need not recruit another spy from the Admiralty to protect my sisters." He said the word spy as though it were a bad word. "I will arrange matters so that I can stay here in London as long as I'm needed."

The baroness smiled benevolently at Benedict.

"I'm so glad you will be able to do that, my dear," she said "I will feel so much better knowing that you are with the girls at all times."

"Rowan," said the baron, "you haven't had your say. What do you think of this arrangement?"

Rowan looked at her father and then at Max.

"If Lord Darby can restrain himself from pulling me from my mount at every opportunity," she said, "I think it's a fine plan. It was difficult to go out before this incident because we were always inundated by young men wishing to attract our attention. If we are seen in the company of Lords Darby and Birmingham on an on-going basis, perhaps some young men will decide that there are young ladies who are equally desirable but more easily approached."

Rowan was very proud of herself for this sensible speech. Then she blushed and mentally kicked herself. She was beyond delighted that she would have time to get to know Lord Darby and see if they would suit.

She also meant what she had said. The overwhelming attention that she and her sisters had attracted, while flattering, was not fun. It made her feel guilty that the men of the ton had focused on the Flame Sisters and were virtually ignoring all the other, very lovely and worthy young ladies who were making their debut this season.

How were she and her sisters to make friends of other young ladies if they were all jealous of them? And she and her sisters definitely wanted to make some new female friends. They had no real acquaintances in London. It would be lovely to have female friends with whom to visit Hatchards, the famous bookstore that seemed to stock every book in the world. And while she loved her sisters, wouldn't it be wonderful to have young women of her own age with whom to discuss their mutual experiences as somewhat older ladies making their come outs? Rowan smiled at her father.

"Excellent!" said the baron. "My dear," he said, turning towards his wife, "do you have anything to add?"

"I think that some sustenance is in order," said the baroness, ringing a small silver bell that was sitting on a side table. "We have much to discuss. I believe our plans will be assisted by a cup of the brew that soothes and some sandwiches and cakes." A footman answering the summons was given the order for a hearty tea.

"Blake dear," said the baroness, "will you be able to stay for tea before returning to your duties?"

"Thank you, Rose," he replied. "I would be delighted to partake of the offerings of your truly outstanding kitchen. I heard that you've recently hired a French pastry chef. How is he working out?"

"*She* is doing very well. You'll see for yourself. Madame Laval recommended her."

"Madame Laval is all that is kind and generous," said Blake. "Since she agreed to take my Mary and our eldest daughters under her wing, they have all been in alt. I had no idea that Madame was so selective about her clientele. Mary had not been able to get Madame's notice until Queen Charlotte intervened! The woman charges the earth, but it's worth it to see my wife and daughters so happy.

"Madame was kind enough to make one or two referrals to me when I escorted the ladies to a fitting. She recommended a particular tailor who is under her guidance. Since I began to give him my custom, I believe that my superiors have begun to take more notice of me," Blake continued.

"When I first visited this tailor, Buchée is his name, he looked at me and told me that my valet was drinking my champagne, rather than using it to shine my shoes. He said that I should sack him before he began to substitute the jewels in my cravat pins. And do you know? When I returned home after my fitting, I checked and damned if two of my pins weren't missing!

"When I confronted my valet, he broke down and told me that he had a gambling problem and had hocked my pins to pay his debts! I dismissed him, but I found a place for him in the country with a friend of mine. Hopefully, away from temptation, he can put his life back together again. He's not a bad man. Just weak. Buchée recommended a young valet — also French — who is the best man I've ever had.

He's industrious, pleasant and helpful! Who knew such a combination of traits was possible in one's valet?"

The baron laughed. "If Hightower, my valet, whose family has worked for the barony for centuries, heard you say such a thing, he would be most insulted! He believes that a valet who is pleasant is falling down on his duties to keep his man up to snuff!"

They all laughed at this, especially the baron's daughters. Hightower, although quite stiff and formal, had always smuggled sweets to them when they were little, and even now treated them with an avuncular air.

The arrival of the tea tray interrupted this discussion of fashion and its devotees. After the cups and plates had been handed around, the family got down to planning escort duties. As Rowan followed the conversation, she wondered if she and Lord Darby would ever be able to have some time alone. She had noticed, during his visit, that he had beautiful lips — full and very mobile. What would it be like to kiss them? And when could she arrange to find out?

*"Max and Rowan's a-mazing adventure
had just begun!"*

# CHAPTER TWELVE
## *What Happens at a Venetian Breakfast ...*

*How will you know if you can find happiness with your future husband, young ladies? You will know by your reaction to his kisses! Kisses come in many different varieties. If he's the right man for you, his kisses will make you feel wonderful. If you don't feel wonderful, he is not the right man for you!*

—*Lady X's Admonitions to Young Women (Third Edition, 1802)*

Max was perplexed. What on God's green earth was a Venetian breakfast? Max thought he had a wide experience of the town, but he could never remember attending, or even being invited to a Venetian Breakfast.

It was the day after what he now thought of as 'the park incident.' Lady Edanmore had sent him, as promised after

a prolonged discussion of her daughters' social schedule,
a list of their social engagements for the next three weeks.
There were annotations about proper dress for each event,
the amount of time that he should allot for each outing and
details about where and when he and Grey were to meet the
young ladies. Benedict and the guards were to be dressed as
footmen. Lady Edanmore had also sent a note thanking him
for his efforts in keeping her daughters safe. Max was really
impressed with the woman he now thought of as his future
mother-in-law.

Max turned his attention to the Venetian Breakfast, which
was to take place in a few days. The baroness had written,

*Lady Fontaine is hosting this event at the family retreat
in Richmond. It will begin at about 1 in the afternoon and
we should arrive no later than 2. There will be a great deal
of food, drink, music, dancing and, weather permitting, boat
races on the estate's very large pond.*

*Lady Fontaine's Richmond retreat is known for its
extensive grounds and gardens that are littered with
picturesque ruins, gazebos and follies. There is also a maze.
Walking in said grounds and gardens is an activity to be
pursued by those wishing some private time without the risk
of impropriety.*

*This event is not a rural frolic. One's finest clothing
and jewelry, suitable for making a morning call, should be
worn. This is also not a breakfast, but more like an on-going,
extremely opulent main meal, supplemented with champagne
and other spirituous liquors. One should note that there is
nothing Venetian about this event. Rather, the term denotes
a type of opulence and, dare I say, hedonism for which the*

*Venetians are supposedly known. Not having been to Venice, I
could not comment on this. Perhaps I can convince the baron
to take me there once the girls are all married.*

*We will go in several carriages from Edanmore House.
I suggest that you and Lord Birmingham ride and meet us
at noon at the front entrance. You should expect to return to
London in the evening by about 10."*

"And that's only one event!" thought Max. "This is going
to be a very long month. Luckily, they don't have any plans
for that evening!"

Lady Fontaine's Venetian Breakfast turned out to be an
event to remember for a number of reasons. The day started
with a surprise. When Max and Grey rode up to Edanmore
House, he found the three sisters all beautifully turned out,
but mounted on their horses. They had decided that morning,
since, as Lily explained, the weather was so fine, that they
would rather ride than be pulled along in a carriage. Benedict
was also mounted on the large grey stallion he'd been riding in
the park. The footmen, all of whom were mounted on powerful
looking bay geldings, rode like cavalry officers. Benedict later
acknowledged that the description was appropriate.

The party made the journey in about 90 minutes. Since
they were accompanied by two large traveling coaches, their
pace was a little slower than it would normally have been, had
everyone been on horseback.

The first carriage held the baron and his wife, the
baroness's friend, Lady Millicent Glendower, Baroness
Highland, who was related by marriage to Bertram Higbee.
He was the recently married youngest Higbee son. Also in
the party was Lord Mortimer Jenkins, Viscount Broadstone, a

widower who was a longtime friend and political colleague of Baron Edanmore. The second carriage was for the return home and was intended to carry the sisters and two of their escorts.

The party arrived at what Lady Fontaine described as her family's rustic retreat at about half past 1. The breakfast was in full swing. An orchestra had been installed on a raised platform and was playing pleasant clearly chosen for listening rather than dancing. Footmen were circulating with glasses of champagne and lemonade. Several long tables dotted the expansive lawn and were groaning under the weight of both sweet and savory offerings.

The guests were gathered in small groups, standing or sitting and talking. A number of the younger guests were playing a game with colored balls, mallets and iron hoops. There seemed to be a serious difference of opinion about the rules, but they all looked like they were having fun.

Another group of young men and women were sitting under a tree while one of them read from a book. The listeners seemed entranced by the reading. Some couples were strolling the beautifully cultivated grounds. In the distance, one could see a folly and a glistening lake.

Lady Fontaine came forward to greet the baron's party.

"My dear baron and baroness," she began, "how lovely that you were able to join us today! Welcome to our little retreat! Did you know, it has no name? Isn't that the silliest thing you ever heard? It's only been in the family for about 200 years, and no one has been able to agree on a name!"

She laughed, a light tinkling sound that encouraged the others to join in her amusement. The baron bowed and introduced the entire party, who acknowledged their hostess with delight.

They walked through the entrance of the maze where the yews soared toward the sky and met to form an arch more than ten feet high. Max sighed. "Alone at last" he thought. "We are together as we were meant to be." He could hear Rowan's sisters and their escorts making their way through the maze. They were certainly a noisy lot!

Max soon discovered that his Rowan seemed to have an uncanny instinct for finding her way through the maze. Whenever they came to a turning point, she would stop and stand quite still. Then she would smile at him and say, "This way," and on they would walk. She had yet to make a mistake.

"She'd be a good spy," Max thought. "Wouldn't it be wonderful to work together as a team?" Then he caught himself and realized what he was thinking. He would hate to have Rowan placed in danger. In fact, since having decided that he would marry Rowan, he had been thinking of resigning his job in the Admiralty and focusing on learning the business of running the earldom. Although his father was in good health and would hopefully live for many years, it was time for Max to pick up some of the work. His father should be able to relax and spend more time on leisure pursuits. "Like visiting his grandchildren," a voice said. "If you act quickly, he could have two or three in a few years!"

"Oh my!" Rowan's voice cut through his musings. "I've managed to get us lost!"

"What did Rowan mean by that?" Max asked himself. And then he thought, "Alone at last!"

Rowan looked at him, a sparkling smile lighting up her eyes. It dazzled him. "If only I could see that smile every day," Max thought.

"There is no fixed plan," she continued, "except for you to enjoy yourselves. We have been blessed with the very best of weather. There are rowboats down at the lake, should anyone care to row, and the orchestra will play some music to dance to later on.

"Perhaps some of the young ladies will entertain us with their various talents. One of my guests actually arrived with her harp in anticipation of such a request! All I require of my guests is that they enjoy themselves today. If there is any amusement that I can offer to make this breakfast more to your taste, you have only to name it, and it will be done if it is in my power to do so."

"We've had such a lovely turn out," Lady Fontaine continued. "The cream of London society is here, so many interesting people."

The baroness looked around her.

"Is that Lady Audington?" she asked, indicating a matron wearing a purple turban with egret feathers. "I've never met her, but a friend pointed her out to me one evening at the opera. I was warned that she is the worst gossip in London."

Lady Fontaine laughed.

"All of the hostesses invite her, but keep an eye on her coming and going. If she's not invited to an event, she fabricates the most outrageous tattle about it. Over the years, we've found that it is wiser to keep her close and minimize the damage."

To Rowan and her sisters Lady Fontaine said, "Watch your steps, young ladies. Lady Audington likes nothing better than to ambush courting couples. Keep an eye out for the egret feathers!"

"Lady Audington and my mother made their come outs together," said Max. "Apparently, she loved to stir the pot even as a young woman. When I came down to town after Cambridge, my mother warned me about her. I'll make sure that the Misses Higbee stay far away."

Lady Fontaine nodded her head and smiled. The baron thanked their hostess for her kindness and hospitality. At her urging, their party moved on to the refreshment tables.

The sisters, escorted by Benedict, Max and Grey and shadowed by their two guards, were given a tour of the grounds by Lady Fontaine's son, Gerard. He was making his own debut of a sort, having recently completed his studies at Oxford. It was obvious that he was fascinated by Ivy. She was very polite and friendly to him as he showed his guests the glories of his family's country home. Rowan and Willow were aware that Ivy was treating him as she would any charming puppy.

Gerard had obviously saved what he considered the best feature of his home for last.

"And here is the maze!" he said with great pride in his voice.

The party gazed at the mammoth yew hedge maze. Gerard explained that it had been designed in the early part of the last century by George London and Henry Wise, the same team that had somewhat earlier created the maze in Hampton Court for William III. While not as large, he explained, this maze was still a challenge.

When Ivy saw the maze, she grinned with glee. She had a love of puzzles, and a maze was a puzzle writ large in three dimensions.

"Let's see how long it will take us to go through the maze," she said. "I'm sure it's going to be an a-mazing adventure!" She smiled slyly at her own pun.

"Wait!" exclaimed Benedict. "If we're going into the maze, we should go together. There's no knowing who might be lurking in there!

"Oh pooh!" said Ivy. "Who is going to harm us in a maze? I'm going in. If anyone wants to join me, please do."

Grey stepped forward.

"I would be pleased to escort you through the maze," he said. They began to walk toward the entrance together, followed by one of their guards.

"I'm going," stated Willow. "Anyone who comes along had better be prepared to keep up with me. I've read all about every maze in England," she announced, "but I've never even heard of this one! I can't wait to see if my theories about solving a maze are correct." She moved quickly towards the entrance. Both Gerard and Benedict hurried to catch up with her, while a second guard followed along.

Max turned to Rowan.

"May I escort you through the maze, Miss Rowan," he asked, offering her his arm.

"I confess to disliking mazes," she responded. "I always feel that there are evil forces lurking in the branches of the hedges. Perhaps holding onto your arm would make me feel safer," she said, with an inviting smile.

Placing her hand on his arm and covering it with his other hand, he gazed into her eyes.

"I shall fight any dragons who dare to interfere with our adventure," Max promised. Did Rowan know, he wondered, that he was promising much more than just a stroll through a maze? That he was promising her his protection for the rest of their lives?

"What are we going to do, Max?" asked Rowan. "We're all alone and lost in the maze!" She was still smiling that inviting, bewitching smile.

"You mustn't be afraid," said Max. "I'll take care of you! Here! Come into my arms! I'll guard you!"

Max drew a very willing Rowan into his arms. She lifted her face to his and looked directly into his eyes. She could hear her sisters' laughter and the murmur of their escorts' voices in the wind as they wended their way toward the center of the maze.

"Max," she whispered.

"My Rowan," he replied. And then he lowered his lips to hers.

At first, her response was slightly restrained, but Max realized that she was not unwilling. It seemed as though she was silently asking him a question. He pulled her deeper into his embrace and increased the pressure of his lips on hers, answering her question. "Yes," he said silently. "You. Only and always and forever you." She sighed and melted in his arms as she responded warmly to his kiss. "You," her lips replied. "Only and always and forever you."

Max and Rowan's amazing adventure had just begun. Time had no meaning. The kiss had no beginning and no end.

Until suddenly, it did.

*"Rowan and her horse moved as one beautifully coordinated being."*

# CHAPTER THIRTEEN
## *Murder! Mayhem!*

*At a time of distress, young ladies, scream at the top
of your lungs! When in trouble, it does not help to faint or
affect a weak aspect! Intelligent young ladies do not carry a
vinaigrette in their reticules. Rather, they carry a sock stuffed
tight with pennies! A well-weighted reticule is a formidable
weapon of self-defense!*

—Lady X's Admonitions to Young Women (Third Edition, 1802)

"Oh my," said a high-pitched female voice. "What have
we here?" It was Lady Audington! Her white egret feathers
fairly shivered in glee at having caught a young couple in a
comprising position.

"Is that you, Maximillian Francis Browning? And with
Miss Rowan Higbee? She looks quite disheveled! What have
you two naughty young people been doing? Didn't your

mother teach you, Max, not to tumble young ladies in a maze? It really isn't the done thing you know," she said archly.

Max bowed to Lady Audington as Rowan hastily tidied her hair.

"You know, Lady Audington," he said, "that I would never take advantage of any young lady. Not even in a maze, where there are so many temptations. You mustn't tease Miss Rowan! You know that there was no tumbling going on! We are a betrothed couple and were doing quite a bit less than betrothed couples do when they find themselves lost in a maze."

At this amazing speech, Rowan dropped her head shyly and blushed, trying with all the acting talent at her disposal, which she admitted to herself was not very much, to imitate a simpering miss.

"Betrothed?" said Lady Audington skeptically. "Your mother did not share this wonderful news with me!"

"It only happened very recently," said Max. "The announcement is still being prepared."

"Well!" huffed Lady Audington, "I shall attempt to keep this news to myself. However, if I don't see the announcement in the paper within 24 hours, I will feel free to tell the world what I saw! You cannot be allowed to ruin this young woman's reputation without consequences," she concluded. She nodded decisively at these words, her feathers bobbing up and down and then turned away. After taking a few steps, she stopped and looked back at them. "You have run into a dead end," she said. "The center of the maze is to the left." She pointed in that direction and then hurried away.

"How long do you think it will be before she tells her most intimate friends that she caught us together in the maze?" asked Rowan in a low voice.

"I'd say about ten minutes," replied Max.

"That was very fast thinking," Rowan said, "but oh dear! Now what? Are we truly committed to becoming engaged?"

"Would that be such a terrible circumstance?" asked Max. "I think that we would get on very well together."

"We hardly know one another!" replied Rowan, while her heart began pounding very quickly. It was true that she had begun to think of Max as a man she might like to marry, but they hadn't spent much time together. Did she really want to enter into a betrothal with him?

"Yes," said a little voice in her mind. "You know you want him. You certainly liked kissing him. More than liked!" As Rowan was distracted by the prompting of her thoughts, Max continued.

"I knew the moment I saw you across the room at Almacks that there would never be anyone other than you for me," he told her. "I've been going mad these past weeks trying to get an introduction to you. I was desperately afraid that you would meet someone other than me, and fall in love with him before I could make your acquaintance!"

"Really?" said Rowan softly. "How could you be sure that we'd suit?"

"My heart told me," Max whispered, putting his lips against her right ear. "Your goodness, your intelligence, your kindness, they all form a bright light that surrounds you. I saw it the first time you walked down the stairway at Almacks. It was as though a blazing star had entered the room. In that moment, I felt that my fate was sealed. I could sense our life together rolling out in front of me."

"That's how it was for you also," Rowan's inner voice reminded her. "You were afraid he would meet someone else and fall in love with her."

Max dropped to one knee. "My dearest, sweetest, most lovely Rowan," he said, "please make me the most fortunate of men and let me be your husband. I vow that you will never have even one moment of regret if you marry me."

Rowan looked down at Max. Did she truly, truly love him enough to commit herself to him for the rest of her life? How could she be sure that her feelings for him were deeper than those she had felt for her first love? She had been deceived by his feelings for her, not by her feelings for him, she realized. How did she feel about Max?

All of a sudden, Rowan's awareness of their surroundings became extremely acute. She held out her hand to Max and urged him to rise.

"Something's wrong!" she whispered urgently.

"What?" he whispered back, confused about the change in the air around them. She had been about to accept his offer of marriage. He was sure of it. Now she was focused on something completely different. What had changed?

"Listen," Rowan said with a great urgency. "What do you hear?"

He listened. "Nothing unusual," he said. "Birds, insects and the wind blowing in the branches."

"Exactly," said Rowan. "Nothing!"

Nothing! Her sisters' happy chatter and their escorts' voices had been a pleasant background for the last fifteen minutes or so. Now there was silence!

Max heard the silence too.

"Come!" he said urgently. Taking Rowan's hand, they began to run along the path. Max had a bad feeling in the pit of his stomach.

"No matter what," said Max to Rowan as they ran, "stay with me! Don't go off on your own! Promise me!" he said urgently.

"I promise," she said, and then, "this way! It leads to the center of the maze!"

"She's amazing," thought Max. "Frightened and running toward trouble, she knows just where to go! What a woman!"

Rowan was right. In the next minute, they broke into a large, open area, the middle of the maze. Max surveyed it in the blink of an eye. A few stone arches, a fountain, some statuary and five men lying on the ground, gaged and tied up. There was no sign of Willow or Ivy. Max and Rowan hurried to the men and began to remove their gags and their bonds.

Before they could ask, Benedict said,

"They were waiting for us. Ten men in black hoods! They were standing quite still, almost like statues. When we first saw them, we thought they had been placed here to scare people who got through to the center of the maze. We laughed, thinking it ridiculous.

"As four of the men suddenly approached Willow and Ivy and threw large cloth bags over them, we realized that this was trouble. The men swept the girls off their feet and carried them off through a hole in the maze before we could respond. The hole is over there. See?"

Benedict pointed toward one of the hedges that had been cut so that an opening could just be seen.

Grey, now able to talk, continued.

"As they were abducting the girls," he continued, "the other men jumped us, gagged us and tied us up. They clearly didn't want to hurt us, but just as clearly, they were focused on rendering us silent and unable to interfere with their plans!"

Evans, one of the soldier footmen who had been serving as a guard, spoke up.

"It was the damnedest thing I ever saw," he said. "Beg pardon for the rough language, miss," he added, acknowledging Rowan. Then he continued. "The maneuver was as precise as any I have ever seen. It was obviously well planned, and they had practiced it until they were absolutely perfect. They were in and away in less than two minutes. I'm so sorry miss," he said to Rowan. "It's only been a few minutes and they can't have gone far. We'll get your sisters back to you safe and sound."

"Did they say anything?" Rowan asked.

Max was amazed at her composure.

"Not a word," said Grey. "They were absolutely silent. They didn't even gesture to one another. Evans is right. It was as if they had planned everything down to the last second and practiced their moves until they were perfect. It was almost like a scene in a play."

Gerard, relieved of his gag and the ropes binding his hands and feet, looked grim and pale as he listened to the account of the disaster.

"But how did they know where we would be?" asked Max. "And how were they able to create the exit in the hedge without anyone knowing about it?"

"The maze is very far from the house," said Gerard. "Even when the family is in residence, no one really comes out here. The grounds men only trim the hedges two or three times a year. The estate is so big that anyone could come in, especially at night or in the early morning and cut through the hedge. It would take a bit of work, but it wouldn't take all that long and it wouldn't make much noise."

"Enough talking," said Benedict, standing up. "We need to let Lady Fontaine know what has happened and to organize a search."

"We need to do so quietly," said Max. "It would be better not to let anyone know that the girls have been taken. Their reputations could be completely ruined if the news should get out. Instead of telling Lady Fontaine right now, let's alert the baron and see what we can do on our own."

Turning to Gerard, who was white as a sheet, he said, "We have your word that you will not tell anyone what has happened?"

"Yes, my lord. Certainly," Gerard responded. "I will do everything in my power to assist you in retrieving the young ladies."

"Let me go through the hole in the maze first," said Max. "I may find a clue to the identity of the abductors and where they went."

"I'll go with you," said Rowan. "I'm sure that my sisters didn't make it easy for their captors, even after they were bundled into the bags. It doesn't sound like they gagged them, so perhaps they made noise," said Rowan.

Max was silent. Rowan gave him a hard look.

"You think that maybe the captors did something so my sisters couldn't hinder them," she stated. "Maybe rendered them unconscious as soon as they had a chance."

"It's a definite possibility," said Max. "We don't know why they took them, but there are some assumptions that can be made. For right now, let's see if we can pick up a trail."

Rowan and Max walked through the opening in the hedge, looking all around for any sign of the passing of the abductors. The others followed them, looking for anything that Max and Rowan had missed. As they came out of the hedge, Max surveyed the ground and pointed.

"There," he said, looking at the flattened grass and the signs of a struggle on the ground. "They went that way," he said, and he pointed toward a stand of nearby trees.

"You go with Miss Rowan," said Grey. "The guards, Gerard and I will go get the horses and bring them to the front gate as quickly as we can."

"Bridles only," said Grey. "We don't want to take the time to saddle all those horses."

"Right," said Max. He and Rowan followed the trail of flattened grass to the edge of the woods. "They would have had a carriage," he said. "I can't imagine that they would have wanted to go any distance with the girls draped over their mounts. Let's see what we can find. You go to the right, and I'll go to the left. Stay in sight. They may be waiting to catch you up as well. I can't lose you!"

Even though she was desperately fearful for her sisters, Rowan couldn't help but marvel at this man, who was treating her like an equal. He was a trained spy. Perhaps he intuited that she had certain abilities that could make her a good partner.

She turned her attention to looking for signs of horses or a carriage. As she made her way over the leafy terrain, she muttered a prayer her maternal grandmother had taught her.

"Make Your sight my sight, make Your wisdom my wisdom, make Your strength my strength so that I may do your work in the world."

Rowan felt as though her grandmother was walking by her side, guiding and strengthening her. Her grandmother had been a wise woman who had lived a very long life. Everyone on Edanmore loved her. When she became ill, her entire family had gathered to care for her.

Rowan had been in her early teens when her grandmother had died. They spent a great deal of time together in those last few days, talking quietly about the family and about special memories that her grandmother wished to share.

At one point, she said, "Look into my eyes." Rowan had done so. Her grandmother seemed to be summoning all her remaining strength. She took Rowan's hands in hers and said, "In our family, we have a gift that is passed from one generation to another. I give this gift to you. For each of us it is somewhat different. You will discover its many treasures as you live your life. Your strength and skill in using your gift will come with your developing belief in yourself.

"In times of doubt or distress, know that I am always with you, watching over you. Know that your Creator is also loving and caring for you. Say this prayer, which I will teach you, and know that you are never alone. Then she had taught Rowan her prayer.

As Rowan walked through the small wood, she added a prayer of her own.

"Please keep my sisters safe and unharmed. Let us find them quickly." She heard Max shout and ran towards him.

"Did you find something?" she asked breathlessly.

"Carriage wheels," he said, pointing to the ground.

Rowan could see the impression on the ground.

"Can we follow them?" she asked.

"They almost certainly will go toward the gate where we can pick up our horses," Max said. "Let's just keep an eye on them as we make our way there, just to be sure that they didn't take a different route out."

Max reached for Rowan's hand and led her through the small forest. He was right. The carriage had been driven right through the front gate. If they used a traveling carriage, anyone seeing it would have thought that it was a guest leaving early. It would have been unremarked.

As they came out of the trees, they saw the men with their horses. Rowan hurried over to her stallion and vaulted onto his back, obviously comfortable riding astride although her skirts rode up and exposed a pair of very shapely limbs.

Max pointed out the carriage tracks to the other men, mounted Sheik and they all galloped away from the estate. One of the guards, who was an expert tracker, led the way, watching the carriage tracks carefully.

One part of Max's mind noted that Rowan and her horse moved as one beautifully-coordinated being.

"How extraordinary she is," he thought.

They had ridden for about 20 minutes when they heard the crashing of some living thing or things through the thick hedges that lined the road. The tracker held up his hand and they all stopped and listened. Human voices!

"My sisters!" shouted Rowan. Before she could ride toward the source of the noise, Max grabbed the reins of her mount.

"Wait!" he whispered urgently. "Someone might be following or tracking them. The last thing we want is to lose you too, or to give them a chance to overcome us, although that's unlikely now that we're prepared."

Max pulled a very lethal looking gun from underneath his jacket. Much to his utter astonishment, Rowan leaned slightly forward and pulled a small lady's pistol from a holster fastened to her right thigh.

"They won't get to me!" she whispered back. "I'm a crack shot even though this pistol looks fairly innocent. My brother Brendon is a genius with anything mechanical. He made some adjustments to this pistol so that it shoots with pinpoint accuracy and delivers a lethal bullet."

"You'll have to tell me more about your family when this is all resolved," said Max. "They seem like an extremely interesting group of people."

"I love my family," said Rowan, "and the word 'interesting' doesn't begin to adequately describe any of them." She smiled. Something in Max's heart melted. He would do anything to have her smile about him in that way, he realized.

Meanwhile, Benedict and the two guards had dismounted and were crouching by the side of the road near the area where all the noise was coming from. The rest of the party stayed mounted and waited for the situation to become clearer. The shouts were becoming louder.

"Mayhem! Murder!"

"Murder! Mayhem!

Rowan couldn't help smiling. Several years before, when the three girls were beginning to prepare for their come outs, their parents had convened what the girls later called the "Murder! Mayhem!" meeting.

Their father had explained that although they all lived simply on Edanmore, his daughters were all heiresses. When they went to London, the sisters would always be somewhat at risk for abduction. They would be well protected, he assured them, but he and their mother felt that they should all learn how to take care of themselves.

One of the easiest ways to defuse a threatening situation, their father had explained, was for a woman to scream at the top of her lungs. He had suggested the words "Murder! Mayhem!" The girls had practiced screaming "Murder! Mayhem!" until they were hoarse — and very pleased with themselves.

Lily and Willow were using the "Murder! Mayhem!" strategy now as they ran through the wooded area, through brambles and bushes. A minute after the waiting group had clearly heard their shouts, the two girls broke out of the thicket and emerged onto the road. Other than being disheveled and having bits of branches and leaves in their hair, Willow and Ivy looked healthy and whole.

Rowan slipped from her mount and ran toward her sisters, throwing her arms around them in relief and welcome. They were both breathing very heavily. As she held them, she saw the soldiers look to Max for guidance. Something unspoken passed between them.

Benedict and the two guards quietly led their horses into the wooded area in the direction from which the sisters had come. Every few steps, they listened closely and then continued. The tracker led the group.

Max, Grey and Gerard had dismounted and had joined the three sisters. Max was the first to speak.

"We need to get away from here," he said, "in case the abductors are following you. Willow, why don't you come up with me and Ivy can ride with Lord Birmingham."

To their credit, thought Max, the girls followed his directions without any fuss. They were quickly mounted astride behind the two men. Max gave Rowan a leg up onto her stallion. They all galloped back to the Fontaine estate.

They came in through a back entrance near the stables and quickly dismounted. All seemed quiet, which suggested that no alarm had yet been sounded.

"We have to get Willow and Ivy into a room in the house where they can repair their hair and clothing. Where shall we go, Gerard?" Rowan asked.

Gerard looked extremely pale and very distressed.

"I'll take you to my sister Anne's room," he said. "She rarely uses it now that she's married, and she isn't here today. Shall I send one of the maids to help?"

"No, but thank you," said Rowan. "The fewer people who see my sisters in their current state, the better."

Gerard led them through the kitchen entrance and up the servants' stairs to his sister's room.

"I'll send my valet to you with water and towels," he said. "He's very discreet and completely devoted to the family. Fifth generation of his family to work for ours."

"Thank you," said Rowan, entering the room with her sisters. Before she closed the door, Max said, "I'll tell your parents that your sisters are feeling headaches coming on and would like to leave as soon as possible. We can bring them up to date on the way home."

"I agree," said Rowan. As she closed the bedroom door, she reflected that Max was an extremely competent man. Everything he did was almost matter of fact. He didn't fuss. Even more important, he didn't fuss about her! He just got on with whatever had to be done. He had trusted her, during the hunt for her sisters, to take care of herself. Truly, he was an unusual man. A little voice in her head said, "And he has such kissable lips and muscular thighs!"

Gerard returned to the door of his sister's room just as Max and Grey were about to find the baron and baroness.

"My valet will be here shortly with all that is necessary," he reported. He looked extremely troubled and was shuffling his feet.

"What does he have to tell us?" Max asked himself. "He's acting like a very guilty man."

Max and Grey exchanged a glance and saw that they had the same thought. Max pulled Gerard into a spare bedroom next to his sister's room. Like Anne's room, it was light, airy and furnished in simple but elegant taste. A large cream and gold floral design Axminster rug covered the floor. The bed was surrounded by pale green hangings. A restful pastoral painting hung above the mantle of the fireplace.

Grey closed the door and Max pushed Gerard up against it and held him there.

"Just spit it out, man," said Grey. "Better to get it off your chest than to brood about it."

"You had something to do with the abduction, I dare say," said Max.

Gerard's head snapped up, and he looked in astonishment at the two menacing men. Consternation and relief were written on his face.

"How did you know?" he asked. "I didn't mean any harm! She said it was a joke and that the girls would not be hurt. She said that it would increase their fame!"

"The kind of fame that comes with being kidnapped is no joke!" said Max sternly. "All the girls, not only Willow and Ivy, would be ruined if word of the abduction were known. The gossips would blow up the story so that it was all three girls, they were gone overnight and were only found in disreputable circumstances late the next day! No decent man would be willing to marry any of them!"

Gerard's face went dead white, and he swayed. Max thought he might actually faint or burst into tears. The boy really didn't know what he had aided and abetted. He was just down from Oxford and obviously didn't have even a hint of ton bronze yet.

"Who put you up to this stupidity?" asked Grey.

"I don't think I can tell you," mumbled Gerard. "Mustn't bandy about a woman's name, you know."

Max grabbed Gerard's cravat and raised him three inches into the air. The boy tried to protest, but he couldn't breathe. Max said slowly and clearly, as though talking to a two-year-old, "You. Will. Tell. Me. What. You. Know."

Gerard obviously believed Max, because, as his face was turning blue, he nodded his head in assent. Max slowly lowered Gerard to his feet and released his stranglehold on the boy's throat. Gerard gasped and coughed as air rushed back into his lungs. Max waited with all the patience at his disposal — admittedly not much — as the young man slowly came back to himself. After a minute or so, he said quietly, "Well?"

"Flavia. Flavia St John. Her brother is Baron Hibbert. Lord Frederick St John. They're cousins. Known them all my life. Their father is Viscount Somersby. The family is completely rolled up. Bankrupt. Both parents are addicted to gaming and can't seem to stop.

"Flavia approached me a few days ago and asked me to help her. She told me that her brother had had an idea to make some money so the family could pay off their creditors and have something to live on. His plan, which she didn't explain, had not worked out. She said that unless she and Frederick could get some money, they would all be turned out of their home.

"The shooting in the park," whispered Grey to Max. Gerard continued.

"Flavia said that Frederick had gotten an even better idea. He knew about the Venetian Breakfast and had discovered that the Flame Sisters would be in attendance. Flavia asked me to lead all the sisters into the center of the maze. Several of her brothers' friends would come upon them and trick them into leaving by a secret exit. Then the men would overcome the sisters, bundle them into a waiting carriage and take them to a nearby cottage.

"Frederick would write a ransom note to their father. When Frederick received the ransom money, the girls would be released. Flavia assured me that the sisters would be unharmed.

Grey could hear Max trying to control his outrage by taking deep, soothing breaths that did not seem to be doing the job. Max was also grinding his teeth, a habit that only asserted itself in times of nearly unbearable stress. Grey realized that Max's control was almost to the breaking point.

Max spoke softly and slowly, with great difficulty.

"In the history of stupidity, there has never been such a monstrously …there are no words! Did you grow up on a desert island devoid of human contact? Were you raised by wolves?"

Max was fighting for control, but, Grey realized, he was losing the battle. It was time to step in before Max went too far.

"Gerard," Grey said evenly. "I'm sorry to tell you that my friend Max here is within a hair's breadth of murdering you. Let me tell you why, while he struggles to regain his self-control."

Gerard lost all color in his face and slowly crumpled to the floor. He buried his face in his hands.

"I've really done it this time," he sobbed. "I always do really addle-pated things. I just don't understand the ton and all its rules. I never want to hurt anyone! I felt so sorry for Flavia and Frederick! Our family has so much, and theirs has always been on the brink of disaster!" He struggled to control his distress.

"I once asked my father to help the family. He told me that he had done so a number of times over the years. As long as the viscount and viscountess kept gambling, there wasn't much that he could do. When Flavia came to me for help, I felt that I couldn't let her down."

A ran of sunlight flashed through the bedroom window, reflecting in a small mirror on the mantle of the fireplace. The room suddenly seemed to be filled with a luminous glow. Max felt as though Rowan's goodness and compassion had entered the room.

Max looked down at Gerard. He had never seen a young man more sunk in misery. He felt a pang of pity for the boy even though it wasn't warranted. What he wanted was to wring his neck. Max sighed. He was about to do something he might regret, but that he knew Rowan would wish him to do.

"Get to your feet, Gerard," said Max. "This is what is going to happen."

With Grey's help, Gerard managed to clamber to his feet and stand with his head raised and his shoulders back. He was trying to meet his fate bravely.

"Some men," said Max, "are not cut out for London society. They are happier elsewhere, in places where they are free to make their own way in the world without the excessive and arbitrary restrictions of society. Such men can lead very happy lives, get married, have children.

"You are not your father's heir, so you have more choices than you realize. I think that you might find India exciting and challenging. I am going to arrange a position for you with the British East India Corporation."

Gerard took a deep breath.

"I would very much like that!" he replied. "I've always wanted to travel and see new places. But after what I've done, why would you help me in this way?"

"If it was up to me," said Max, "I would happily murder you, feed the pieces to the wolves and then go after your cousins. However, Miss Higbee would not approve. She would wish me to be compassionate and try to help you."

He turned to Grey and sighed.

"Being in love is hell."

Grey struggled to suppress a smile. Poor Max was really

done for. Max continued.

"Pack your things and get ready to go, Gerard," said Max. "I will try to keep your part in this between us, but Flavia and Frederick may talk once their deeds are revealed."

He took his card out of his jacket pocket, wrote his address on the back, and handed it to the young man.

"Meet me at noon tomorrow at this address. I will have arranged your employment and your passage out of England to India. The sooner you put England behind you, the better. When Baron Edanmore hears about this escapade, and he will, though not from me if I can prevent it, he will find it difficult to restrain himself from killing you. He has eight sons, all of whom have great influence. They will also wish to kill you. They will all certainly wish to come after you. Better to be gone before they do so."

Gerard took a long breath.

"Thank you, my lords," he said. "Both of you. I appreciate your help. One day I'll return, having made my fortune, and I will repay you in full."

"Repay us by living a good life and helping others less fortunate than yourself. There will be many opportunities to do so in India," said Grey.

"I will, my lords," said Gerard. "I vow I will." He turned, opened the door and hurried to his room to begin his preparations for his new life.

Max turned to Grey.

"Let's make sure that the absence of the sisters has not been noted," he said.

The two men walked onto the terrace of the bedroom and looked out over the lawn. Max immediately noticed Rowan.

She was standing with her parents and speaking with them, apparently completely at ease. As Max and Grey watched, they saw Willow and Ivy come out of the house arm in arm. They joined their parents and sister and began to chatter in an entirely normal way. Max and Grey hurried out of the spare bedroom and went to catch up with them.

"Are you all right?" Max asked Willow and Ivy quietly, once they were all standing together.

"The girls were just saying that they are a little fatigued. They are not used to so much excitement," responded the baroness. "We were just saying that perhaps it is time to begin the journey home. This is a busy week, and we wouldn't want any of the girls to become overtired."

"An excellent idea," said Max. "Grey and I will certainly be happy to escort you. Benedict and the footmen who were with the girls all day will join us along the way."

The baroness' lips twitched just slightly.

"Thank you for letting us know, my lord," she said.

"It would give me great pleasure if you and your husband would address me as 'Max,'" he said.

"I'm Grey," said his friend.

The Baron and Baroness both smiled. "It would be an honor, gentlemen," they said.

The entire party went to bid farewell to their host and hostess. As the baron was leading his ladies to their carriage, Max said to Lord and Lady Fontaine, "Young Gerard has news to relay to you. Should you have any questions, please apply to me or Lord Birmingham in London. You may rely on our discretion. We will be of help in any way that we can."

His host and hostess looked somewhat puzzled but thanked them and wished them a safe journey back to town. He turned and walked quickly to his waiting mount. Within a few minutes, the carriage and their outriders were through the gates of the estate.

It might have been Max's imagination that he heard the baron's roar from several horse lengths away. He assumed that the sisters were filling their parents in on their misadventure. At one point, the carriage slowed down, as though instructions were being given to the coachman, but the coach did not turn around and quickly resumed a rapid pace. Max took a deep breath. There were still miscreants to bring to justice in London. He and Grey were just the men to do it!

*"Your house would be an ideal facility
on which to experiment."*

# CHAPTER FOURTEEN
## *Untangling a Tangled Web ...*

*Communication is essential for good relationships, young ladies. Do not assume your thoughts and feelings are clear to a person for whom you may care. Very few people are mind readers. Talk to one another! You will thank me for this advice!*

—*Lady X's Admonitions to Young Women (Third Edition, 1802)*

Once back in London, Max and Grey, without stopping to rest or change their clothes, focused on hunting down Flavia and Frederick. Max and Grey now understood that she and her brother were behind both the shooting and the kidnapping of Willow and Ivy. Their first two plans having been thwarted, they might do something truly desperate. The pair had to be apprehended before they tried anything else.

The two friends rode directly to the home of Viscount Somersby, located on the very fringe of Mayfair. The building had a rather neglected look about it. The plantings on either side of the house were in need of weeding. The curtains were drawn over all the windows, as though the household was in mourning. The brass knocker on the front door was dull from want of polishing.

Max knocked several times. Then he and Grey waited. After several minutes, an elderly man in a shiny black coat opened the door. He stared at them as though he was unused to welcoming callers.

"We are here to see the viscount," announced Grey.

"Ain't here," said the servant.

"We will see the viscountess," responded Max.

"Not at 'ome," countered the servant.

"We would be very happy to call upon his son or daughter, in that case," said Grey.

"Ain't no one at 'ome," replied the man.

"I am Birmingham," said Grey in his most aristocratic voice. He handed the man his card. "We have urgent business with a representative of the family."

"No one 'ome," repeated the servant. He began to close the door.

Max inserted his foot into the opening, and he and Grey pushed their way into the hall, brushing the servant aside as they did so. They took a moment to look around.

The hallway had not been properly swept or dusted in some time. There were dust mice in the corners of the room, and a light film of dust lay on shelves empty of the objects that would have once been displayed there.

"Probably sold," thought Max. He and Grey looked at one another and listened carefully for noises in the cavernous entranceway.

They could hear the sounds of quick steps and objects being shoved around. The noise seemed to be coming from the next level of the house. The servant ran to the foot of the stairway and tried to block Max and Grey from going further into the house.

Max pulled a crown out of his pocket and handed it to the old man.

"We'll take it from here," Max said. The old man stepped aside and shuffled away. Max and Grey bolted up the stairs in the direction of the commotion.

Having reached that floor, they began to throw open doors. All the rooms were empty of furniture. The sounds were getting louder. They stopped and listened.

Grey and Max could hear voices raised in agitation. Max motioned in the direction of the sounds with a nod of his head. Grey, understanding the signal for silence and stealth, nodded in agreement. They made their way quickly and quietly toward the room from which the noise was coming.

The door to the room was slightly ajar. Max and Grey stopped to listen in order to assess the situation. Max drew a small pistol from the pocket of his jacket. Grey did the same. Then they moved as close to the opening of the door as they could without being seen.

"What were you thinking?" It was the voice of an older man raised in anger.

"We were trying to help you and mother, papa." A young woman's voice.

"But Flavia! To shoot at them in the park! What if you'd actually hurt one of them?" An older woman's voice.

"I was to run to their rescue!" A young man's voice with something of a whine. "No one got hurt!"

"And to hire your worthless friends to abduct them, Frederick! The girls might have been injured! Their reputations could have been ruined!"

"And to involve your cousin Gerald, when his father has been so good to us! "How could you? We shall all be ruined!" The older woman was sobbing.

"But the creditors! How were you ever going to get out from under all the debt? There is nothing left to sell," responded Frederick. "I just wanted to help! To let you know that you could count on me!"

"Some help!" thought Grey.

"We had decided to take up my sister's offer to have us all come to live with her in Cornwall," the older woman explained. "We have been making plans to do so for the last month. That's why we've been selling everything in the house. Not to pay debts, but to raise some money so that we wouldn't come to her empty handed."

"My brother set aside 2,000 pounds for each of you when you were born," the older man explained. "He has managed those funds all these years. They are in trust for you. You were to get the funds when you were ready to set out on your own. There was no way that we could touch those funds. By now, they are worth considerably more than the original amount. Your uncle wanted to make sure that no matter what happened to us, the two of you would have some security."

Max heard the younger woman began to cry. "Father," she said, "why didn't you tell us? We've been mad with worry ever since our 13th birthday. We could see that things were getting worse and worse. We just wanted to help! Why didn't you tell us what you planned?" cried Flavia.

"Your father and I wanted to spare you worry," said their mother. "We wanted to have everything in place when we told you about our plans."

Max and Grey looked at one another, fascinated by this exchange.

"What about us? Are you planning for us to go to Cornwall, too?" asked Frederick.

"No," said their father. "There is nothing there for you. Your mother and I have arranged for you to work as the private secretary to our friend Lord Peterson. We know that you read all about the political doings of the nation. We thought that working with such a prominent member of the House of Lords would help you learn about politics firsthand. Perhaps in time you might run for a seat in the House of Commons. You will live in his home, and he will supply you with a small stipend."

"I would like that very much," said Frederick.

"What about me?" asked Flavia.

"Your great aunt Olivia has agreed to have you come to her as a companion. Next year, she will sponsor another season for you. She'll enjoy having your company, and you can learn a great deal from her about how to navigate the ton."

"I would have liked that excessively," Flavia said in a soft voice. "Great aunt Olivia is a dragon, but she has a warm heart.

"Oh lord!" said Frederick. "What have we done? We've ruined all your plans for us! Baron Edanmore will have us arrested for abducting his daughters if he finds out what really happened! We're ruined! Whatever are we to do?"

Max and Grey had heard enough. They pocketed their weapons. It was clear that the young people had acted on their own and very stupidly. Perhaps there was a way to salvage the situation. Max opened the door and he and Grey walked into the room.

"Darcy and Birmingham at your service," he said as the heads of all four family members turned in astonishment.

"Ruined!" cried Frederick, lowering his face into his hands. His sister gasped and turned pale. She staggered toward a chair and fell into it.

An older man and woman sat beside one another on a settee near the unlit fireplace. They were simply dressed and looked more like tradespeople than a viscount and his viscountess.

"My lords," said their father. "Am I correct in assuming that you have been listening at the door and are aware of some of our sad circumstances?"

"We are indeed aware of all of your sad circumstances," said Grey.

"We came to exact justice," said Max.

The viscountess gasped and said, "No!" in a high, thready voice.

"From what we have just heard," continued Grey, "it is clear that your children acted to protect your family."

"Are you aware of anyone else who was involved?" asked Flavia tentatively.

"Gerard confessed all," said Max.

"Oh, poor Gerard!" wailed Flavia. "Is he going to be arrested?"

"She really is worried," thought Max.

"No," he said. "Gerard understands that what he did was very wrong. As a result of his actions, we are sending him into exile."

"Oh, my lords," said Frederick. "Please don't send him away! He's really a good lad. He only wished to help us. Send us away instead if you must!"

Max and Grey were reluctantly impressed with the young man.

"Actually," Max said, "Gerard is not unhappy with his punishment. He is going to go to work for the East India Company. He leaves for the Far East tomorrow."

"Oh!" said Flavia. "He'll like that! He always wanted to travel, but his father always kept him under his thumb."

"That's more or less what Gerard told us. I think he'll do very well out East," said Grey.

"But what's to become of us?" asked Frederick. It did not escape Max's notice that the young peoples' parents were silent. Maybe there was hope for the family yet.

"What do you think?" Max asked Grey.

"Luckily, the Higbee sisters were able to free themselves and were not missed at the Venetian Breakfast," said Grey. "They weren't gone very long. No one will hear about your foolish prank. However, I think that the baron and his daughters are owed an explanation and a profuse apology in person."

"Very wise," agreed Viscount Somersby. "Very wise indeed. I will write to the baron immediately and ask to meet with him first thing tomorrow. We will all call upon him. I think it would be most appropriate for him to decide what is to be done with us."

"I agree, my dear," said his wife. "It is said that he is a reasonable man. We can only hope that he will be kind to us in our difficult circumstances."

"We will be at that meeting," said Max. "The earl and I can tell him of the conversation we just overhead.

"Thank you, my lords," said the viscount. "I will ask for a meeting at 11 in the morning and will send a note to you once the baron has consented to see us."

And thus it was that a large group of people were gathered in the study of Edanmore House at 11 o'clock the following morning. In addition to the viscount's entire family, there were Gerard's parents, Rowan, Willow and Ivy and Lords Birmingham and Darcy. Gerard was absent, having already left for the docks to begin his new career.

When everyone was settled, the baron spoke.

"This is quite a mess. It is only because I have the three most intrepid daughters in the kingdom, if not in the entire world," he said proudly, "that no harm has come to them or their reputations. However, the actions of your children," he glowered at the viscount and viscountess, "are beyond the pale. There must be serious consequences for their behavior."

"We are all prepared your judgement, my lord," said the viscount, resignation in his voice.

The baron continued.

"I have bought up your vowels, both those incurred by you, viscount, and by your wife. Every. Single. One." The viscountess gasped.

The baron glanced at her. "Indeed," he said.

"I have also acquired the bills outstanding from your creditors and paid them off. From what Darby and the earl have told me, your plan to ruralize with your relatives did not include paying off your debts of honor or paying off your creditors. The sum owed is quite impressive. Almost 10,000 pounds."

The viscountess began to weep silently, dabbing her eyes with a much-mended square of linen.

"The baroness and I have discussed a plan of action. We included our daughters in the deliberation, since it is they who were most affected by what happened. This is what we have decided," said the baron.

"Your plan to run off to the country is not acceptable to any of us. It sets a terrible example for your children. They must learn that problems must be faced and dealt with.

"We have consulted with our son Brian, the architect who refurbished this house, and his wife, who created the interiors. For some time, they have had a project in mind, but had not had a suitable property for their plans.

"They wish to take an older house that is very much in need of repair and see how it might be modernized on a relatively modest budget. They believe that your house would be an ideal facility on which to experiment."

The viscountess gasped. The baron continued.

"They would also like to do these renovations while a family is in residence. Most people cannot vacate a house for a year or more while renovations are being done. They would like to see how various construction and design methods could be altered from the standard way of working, so that a family could stay in place while changes were being made. It would be very helpful if the family would give the architect and designer suggestions as the work went along.

The baron paused and cleared his throat.

"Here is our plan. Your daughter and son will take up the positions you have arranged for them. It strikes us all that they will benefit from seeing a little more of the world and of society. You, viscount and the viscountess, will remain in your home and permit our son and daughter-in-law to move forward with their project. They would appreciate your suggestions, not only about work methods, but about what you would both find decoratively attractive and appealing within the budget that I will establish.

The baron continued.

"I will fund the project, staff the establishment so that it runs as smoothly as possible, and cover the household expenses until the project is completed. Brian and his wife believe that the work should be completed within a year and a half. They hope that, when they are finished, the actual time necessary to completely refurbish an old house will be less than nine months. Because they will be working on a variety of different ways of doing things, the initial project will take considerably longer."

"What do we have to do?" asked the viscount.

"You will make over the deed to the house to me," said the baron. "I will hold it against your debts. You and your wife will live there during the entire project with no cost to yourselves. In addition, you will both pledge never to gamble again. Not in any way.

"I am aware that you have a small income that would allow you to live modestly in your home if you were not gaming. During the time of the construction, if you agree, I will match that amount, and my son, Brian Higbee-James, who is known throughout the ton as something of a wizard with investments, will manage both your funds and my matching funds. At the end of the project, you should have more money on which to live comfortably. If you wish, Brian will continue to help you invest your funds and live on the interest, so that you will have financial security.

"After the project is completed," explained the baron, "the house will be sold. The money that results from the sale will pay off your remaining debt to me and go toward defraying the cost of the renovation. At that time, you may go where you wish.

"This arrangement is contingent upon neither of you gaming in any way. If either of you place a wager of any kind during this project, I will evict you from the house. Your name will be ruined. Your son will lose his position with Lord Peterson and it will be virtually impossible for Flavia to make a decent match.

"I have arranged to have you barred from all establishments where gambling takes place. Understand that you may not engage in even the smallest wager at a house party, or a bet on which raindrop will reach the bottom of a window pane first."

The viscount and the viscountess looked extremely grave.

During all of this, Flavia and Frederick had listened quietly. When the baron concluded his speech, Flavia ran to her mother and embraced her.

"Do you think you and father really can change?" she asked.

The viscountess embraced her.

"We must," she said. "For your sake and for Frederick's future."

The viscount stood and approached the desk where the baron was sitting.

"Your kindness gives me hope that the viscountess and I can put our lives back on a firm footing. You have relieved us of financial worry for the present, and given us the possibility of better days to come. We never really wanted to move to Cornwall. I vow that you will not regret this day's work."

"My sister and I were always like oil and water," confided the viscountess to Flavia.

"Go home," said the baron, "and attend to settling your children in their new situations. Brian and his wife will call upon you tomorrow morning. Broderick will come by in the afternoon to speak with you about the financial and legal details. The baroness and I wish you well."

Frederick, who had been quiet all this time, finally found his voice. He addressed the baron.

"Why are you willing to go to so much trouble and expense to help people you don't know, my lord?" he asked. "People who have tried to take advantage of your daughters? It doesn't make sense."

The baron took a deep breath before answering. When he spoke, he looked straight into the boy's eyes.

"The Higbee family motto is Généreux. Prosprete. Pais. Generosity. Prosperity. Peace. When all people have what they need, not only to survive but to thrive, everyone benefits."

The baron stood and came out from behind his desk. He

extended his hand to the viscount.

Everyone else stood. The baroness escorted the viscount, his wife and their children out of the room and closed the door behind her.

"Now then," said the baron turning to Max and Grey, "there is another matter to discuss."

*"This is really and truly love."*

# CHAPTER FIFTEEN
## *Betrothed at Last!*

*"Love is a precious gift, young ladies. When true love comes to you, embrace it with all your heart. Lust — don't faint my dears, lust is important in a relationship — does not last, although it is quite a lovely experience. But love! True love! True love grows and deepens with every passing day. It stands the test of time and the difficulties that are part of every life. Even when you and your beloved are old and grey and can do little more than sit together and hold hands, true love will sustain and strengthen you. If you find true love, grasp it to your heart and never let it go!"*

—*Lady X's Admonitions to Young Women (Third Edition, 1802)*

Rowan's father turned to look at her.

"Your mother will return in just a moment," he said. Then he looked at Rowan's sisters and at Benedict. "We would like you to remain for this. As you are all unmarried, it will likely be instructive." He turned to Grey. "You may stay or go as you wish," he said.

Grey looked at Max, who had a good idea what was coming. Max said, "You might as well stay, Grey. We've been together in everything else. Why stop now?"

Grey smiled and nodded. Just then, the baroness returned and took her seat by the baron's side. Looking at Rowan and Max, she spoke.

"It took Lady Audington five minutes to get around to congratulating us on the betrothal of our daughter, Miss Rowan Higbee, to Viscount Darby, heir to the Earl of Bainbridge. 'Such a wonderful match my dear. You both must be in alt, especially since the girl has such a paltry dowry!'"

The baroness imitated Lady Audington's high-pitched voice perfectly. "Needless to say, Rowan, we accepted the lady's congratulations with perfect dignity."

"What the blazing bluebells!" shouted Benedict, jumping up out of his seat. "I'll kill him! How dare he? He hasn't even come to see you about courting Rowan, has he father?"

The baron turned to his son. "Sit down, sir, and learn. You are too quick to take offense. What would you do if you felt that a horse had acted badly? Shoot him? You know better! There will be no duels and no killing! I'm sure that Viscount Darby has a very good explanation for Lady Audington's surprising statement." Turning toward Max, the baron asked, "Don't you?"

Max stood.

"My lord," he began. "It has been my wish since the very moment I saw Miss Rowan across the room at Almacks, to call upon you to ask your permission to court her. The overwhelming popularity of all three of your lovely daughters made it impossible to get an introduction to her. I did not want to be among the throngs of gentlemen who were inundating you with offers for her hand even before meeting her."

"Very right and proper thinking," murmured the baroness in an aside to her husband. Her husband nodded in agreement.

Max continued.

"The seeming attack on the young ladies in the park, unfortunate as it was, made that introduction possible. If anything, Miss Rowan's intrepid behavior on that day made me admire her even more. Not only is she lovely, but she possesses character and initiative beyond measure. I truly cherish those qualities in her.

"Quite right," said her mother, nodding her head. "It's very refreshing to meet a gentleman who recognizes what is important in a young lady's character."

Rowan spoke up.

"Ever since the viscount and the earl have been acting as our escorts," she said, "I have gotten to know them both." She blushed. "They are both men of outstanding character. Viscount Darby and I have developed a tendresse for one another," she said softly, smiling.

Max looked at her and returned her smile.

"I felt that I should wait to speak with you, sir, until the situation regarding potential harm to your daughters was resolved," explained Max. "I hoped that Miss Rowan might gain an appreciation of my character as we spent time together. After all, while it was clear to me that we belong together, I could not be sure if she, on such brief acquaintance, could feel the same way."

The baron nodded. "Go on," he said. "I have the picture of how your relationship began to develop. However, it is not clear how Lady Audington came to the conclusion that you and my daughter are engaged."

Rowan and Max looked at one another. Her parents, noticing the look, both smiled.

"There is no other way to say this," said Max. "Lady Audington came upon us in an embrace in the maze. It was entirely my fault. Your daughter is so lovely. It was the first time that we had been alone. She smiled at me, and I was lost," he said.

"No," said Rowan. "It was my fault! I encouraged Max to kiss me. I knew that he would do it if he understood that I wanted him to do so. It was my fault! It was perfectly innocent. How could we know that Lady Audington would come along? It was just bad timing!"

"There is no issue of fault, said the baroness. "It has been clear to anyone with eyes, except perhaps for Benedict, that the two of you have been developing tender feelings for one another. You found yourselves lost in the maze, though how that is possible, given Rowan's uncanny sense of direction, I'm sure I don't know," the baroness said with a twinkle in her eye. "The magic of the maze drew you together and you kissed. That is what happened, was it not?" The baroness addressed this last question to Max.

"Exactly," he said.

"It was magical," sighed Rowan. They smiled lovingly at one another.

Benedict rolled his eyes and shook his head.

Willow and Ivy were following this discussion with rapt attention. When Rowan said "It was magical," they sighed as one in delight. To them, this was the height of romance, devoutly to be wished.

"So, you kissed," said the baron. "I assume that there was some playing with hair involved so that you both had a rather tousled look when Lady Audington came upon you?" His tone of voice was dry.

"Exactly," said Max, although a slight flush had come to his cheeks. He was a little embarrassed by the baron's plain speaking.

"And she probably accused you of much worse than a passionate kiss?" continued the baron.

"As if we would do such a thing in a maze!" responded Rowan, although she privately thought that the center of a maze, perhaps at twilight, might be a perfectly lovely place to do more than kiss.

"And you, viscount, felt the need to explain your actions by announcing that the two of you were engaged?" asked the baron.

"Yes, sir," said Max, "although I proposed marriage to Miss Rowan as soon as Lady Audington had departed."

"And how did my daughter respond?" asked the baroness.

"I didn't," said Rowan. "We became aware that something was wrong and rushed to find my sisters. You know the rest."

The baron turned to Max.

"There is no reason for you to marry my daughter in order to preserve her reputation," he said sternly. "I understand that you acted honorably in accordance with the traditions of the ton. Lady Audington is a terrible gossip and unfortunately, once she saw the two of you in a disheveled state, the horse, as the saying goes, was out of the stable."

"Indeed," said the baroness, "I noticed that she spoke with three of four other people before she made her way to us with her congratulations."

"Of course, he has to marry her!" protested Benedict. "If he doesn't, Rowan will be ruined and so will Willow! And Ivy!"

Willow and Ivy looked at their parents with concern. "Is that true?" asked Willow.

"Rowan mustn't marry the viscount unless she loves him!" protested Ivy. "If she doesn't want to marry him, she can go away and live in a beautiful tower in Venice and wait for her own true love!"

"Mother," protested Benedict, "what is this girl reading? Surely her mind would be improved with a volume of Fordyce's Sermons! Towers in Venice indeed!"

The baroness's light laughter broke the tension.

"No one in this family is going to be sent away, and no one is going to marry anyone but her — or his" she said with a sharp look at Benedict — one true love. That has been the creed of the Higbee family from generation to generation.

"Should Rowan and Viscount Darby wish to marry, I would certainly give my blessing," said the baron. "How do you feel, my dear?" he asked his wife.

"I think it is a very suitable match, but only if they are truly in love," responded the baroness.

"Yes," said the baron. "Only if they are truly in love, and truly wish to marry. That, of course, is what is most important." He smiled at his wife.

Turning to Max, he said, "I believe that you and Rowan should have some time to speak privately with one another."

Looking at Rowan he said, "Why don't you take the viscount into the parlor? Please leave the door open. You may have ten minutes to decide what the two of you would like to do."

Rowan and Max stood. Max said, "Thank you, sir, ma'am," with a slight bow to Rowan's parents. Extending his arm to Rowan, the two left the room together. For a moment, there was silence.

"I think there will be time to have the banns called before they get completely out of hand," said the baroness to her husband. He nodded and smiled, then turned to his daughters. "What do you girls have to say?" he asked.

"She loves him so much!" said Willow. "Anyone can see that!"

"It's so romantic!" sighed Ivy. "Do you think that she will let us be her attendants at the wedding?

Their mother smiled. "I'm sure she will. Madame Laval will be over the moon when she gets the order to design Rowan's bridal clothing and trousseau, as well as new garments for the entire family."

"Please mother, can I wear a color other than white?" asked Ivy.

"We will have to consult Madame Laval about the color scheme for the wedding. Otherwise, we'll never hear the end of it. I'm sure we will all wear colors more interesting than white," replied their mother.

"Maybe she'll let me wear passion-flower pink, mused Ivy. "That color sounds so exotic!"

"All this talk about clothing is irrelevant! How can you let Rowan marry him, father?" growled Benedict. "I think he's a scoundrel, and he's a spy! Do we really need another spy in the family?"

"Blake is not a spy," said the baroness sharply. "He is a highly placed official in the Home Office." She punctuated this remark with a lift of her eyebrows.

"Fine," said Benedict. "Blake is not a spy. But this Max person certainly is. Do you really think he's an appropriate match for our Rowan, Father?"

"I don't see why not," replied his father. "He's financially stable. Broderick approves of him. His father's estate is very well run and he's got a prosperous estate of his own in Cornwall."

Benedict sighed. Reluctantly he said, "He keeps a very fine stable."

"High praise indeed, coming from you," replied his father with a smile. "It seems a suitable match to me. and they are obviously smitten with one another."

"I hope Rowan will realize it," said her mother. "That unfortunate experience when she was younger left her somewhat unsure about her feelings."

The baron nodded. "I put my money on the viscount," he said. "He seems like the determined sort. Not one to let something he wants slip away without a good fight."

The baroness smiled in agreement.

Meanwhile, in the parlor, Rowan and Max were standing in the middle of the room staring at one another.

"Your family is really quite remarkable," he said. "I think you would like my family as well. They are warm and sensible people. There is no question in my mind that they will love you as much as I do."

"Oh Max!" Rowan said, her voice trembling. "There's something I must tell you! It's awful! I didn't want to say anything about it to you, but I must reveal this before we go any further!"

She started to speak slowly and haltingly.

"I was 16. There was a boy. I thought I loved him. I thought he loved me and wanted to marry me. Then I found out he was betrothed to another! I'm so sorry!" Rowan began to cry.

Max drew her into his arms and stroked her hair. "Hush, my love," he said. "You have such a warm and open heart. It would surprise me if there hadn't been at least one young man who had wanted you before I came along. Whatever passed between you, it has nothing to do with us. We will build a life together looking to the future, not to any sadness in the past."

"Oh Max!" Rowan said, pulling slightly away from him and looking into his warm, dark- brown eyes. She had the errant thought that she could curl into those eyes and live there, warm and safe, forever.

"We never. I didn't. I might have agreed to if he'd stayed longer, but..." She couldn't bring herself to tell Max the complete truth: that she was still a virgin, but that she was not completely untouched. Laying her head against his chest, tears flowing down her cheeks, Rowan willed Max to understand.

Max smiled at her gently, all the love in his heart overflowing.

"It truly wouldn't matter to me, my love," he said, "but I understand. There is nothing to judge and nothing to forgive. Whatever happened, it doesn't matter.

"Really?" murmured Rowan through her tears. "Most men wouldn't feel that way!"

Max pulled his handkerchief from his jacket and began to dry Rowan's tears.

"I'm not most men, my love," said Max.

Dropping to one knee, he looked up into Rowan's lovely face.

"Will you marry me, my sweetest, most lovely, brilliant Rowan?" he asked. "I will do everything in my power to give you the moon."

Rowan looked down at him, put her forefinger on his lips and smiled gently.

"I don't want the moon, my love," she said. "I just want you. You and perhaps half a dozen children would make my life perfect!"

Max rose, chuckling.

"Since you come from such a large family, six children is a paltry number," he said. "Do you think your parents would demand more from us?"

"I love my parents very much," said Rowan. "I would like to please them, if we can," she said a little shyly. A faint blush had risen to her cheeks.

Max swung his beloved in a huge circle. Her feet left the ground and she felt like she was flying. She laughed with love and happiness.

"Oh Max," asked Rowan, "Is this really love?

Max hugged Rowan truly happy for the first time in his life. He knew that he was holding all that was precious, all that he would ever need, safe in his arms. His heart was overflowing with gratitude and delight.

"Yes, my dearest Rowan," he said just before his lips claimed hers. It was the kiss that would begin their lives together.

"This is really and truly love."

And so, it was.

The Beginning

*"The marriage of the radiant
Miss Rowan Higbee ..."*

# EPILOGUE

***The Ton Reporter***
***Exclusive!***
***Marriage of the Season!***
***Miss Rowan Higbee Marries Viscount Darby.***
by S. J. Roberts, Society Reporter

*The marriage of the radiant Miss Rowan Higbee, daughter of Baron and Lady Edanmore, sister of the lovely Misses Willow and Ivy Higbee, to Lord Maximillian Francis Browning, Viscount Darby, heir to the Earl of Bainbridge, took place yesterday at St George's Church, Hanover Square.*

*The bride's sisters served as attendants. In accordance with family custom, both of the bride's parents walked their daughter down the aisle and presented her to the groom. Lord Richard Grey Birmingham, the Earl of Wellesly Glen, stood up with the groom. Also standing up with the groom were the bride's eight brothers, a formidable phalanx!*

*The entire party was dressed by Madame Celeste Laval, the ton's most exclusive modiste. Madame Laval recently opened a new salon, "Laval for Gentlemen," which is adjacent to her premises for ladies on Bond Street. Illustrations of the wedding party's fashions follow this article, provided by Madame Laval with permission of Baron Edanmore.*

*The sun shone and a gentle breeze blew as family and friends gathered to see the happy couple united. Invitations to the nuptials themselves were restricted to 300 of the family's inner circle and close friends, who filled the cozy sanctuary to capacity.*

*More than 600 guests attended the wedding breakfast at Edanmore House. It is said that even the dear Queen made a surprise appearance to wish the couple well. It is widely-known that the baron's third son, Mr. Broderick Sean Higbee-James, the noted financier, is a trusted advisor to the Crown.*

*The happy couple left immediately after the final champagne toast had been offered by the bride's father, for a wedding journey to the groom's magnificent estate in Cornwall. After a month there, they plan to tour the continent.*

*While one Flame Sister is married, there are two other beautiful young women looking for love. Gentlemen of the ton, gird your loins and enter the fray! The Misses Willow and Ivy are beyond compare! The men who gain their notice will be truly fortunate! Which one of the Baron Edanmore's daughters will be the next to be struck by Cupid's arrow? Only time will tell!*

*The Edanmore Chronicles Continue!*

**Bedlam in Bath: Ivy's Story — Book 2**
**Chaos in Cardiff: Willow's Story — Book 3**

# AUTHOR'S NOTES

I've always wanted to write a story about a couple who see one another across a crowded room and instantly fall in love. That's because I met my beloved in exactly that way. While it took us some years to actually get together, we were, after all, in our very early teens when we first met, it was, nevertheless, at least for my husband-to-be, love at first sight. It took me a little longer to get with the program. My philosophy of life at that time was, "So many men, so little time." (But only in the most innocent way!)

When we finally got married, our pledge to one another was not to "love, honor and obey," but rather to support one another to realize our individual gifts. My husband has always been my most constant cheerleader and I have been his.

When I was writing Rowan's story, I spent a long time thinking about how it is that we sometimes have a deep knowing about something, but that it can take quite a while for everything to fall into place. This book is a perfect example of that phenomenon.

I have a photograph of myself sitting at a typewriter when I was about three years old. I've been writing ever since. Although I've written and published a wide variety of material over the years, I always wanted to write novels. For some reason I was unable to do so until, finally, finally, whatever had been blocking my process vanished.

One night, I had a dream about a man who turned into a raven. I woke up and immediately wrote down the entire outline of the story. That was my first novel, *The Curse of the Ravenscrofft Brides*. It was the beginning of my new career as a writer of Regency Romances.

*Anarchy at Almacks* is the first of my romances to be published. My heart is singing with happiness and a sense of accomplishment. To every single person reading these words, I urge you to follow your passion. It's really worth it. The journey may not roll out in the way that you imagine it will, but that doesn't matter. What is important is to believe in yourself. Surround yourself with people who believe in you and friends who think you're wonderful. A happy ending is worth working for. And everyone deserves a happy ending.

## A few words about the Isle of Edanmore

Several years ago, before Covid, I saw a posting on Facebook asking former residents or descendants of residents of Arranmore Island to come back and settle on the island.

Arranmore is an island off the west coast of County Donegal in Ulster — Northern Ireland. The local government was heavily investing in internet infrastructure so that people could live on the island and work remotely. As of 2022, the population was 478 people.

I love the idea of spending time in remote places. Although we are not of Arranmore descent, I called my husband and said, "We have to move there!" My husband suggested that perhaps we might try a short visit first.

We have yet to visit Arranmore, but the idea of a small, sparsely populated island off the coast of Ireland stayed with me. What would it be like to be the primary titled landowner on an island like that? How would that family relate to the rest of the population? Would they live a life cut off from everyone else, or might they have a sense of responsibility for the rest of the inhabitants? Could such a place be a utopia of sorts where everyone had enough to eat, access to education, meaningful work to do, good healthcare and long, happy lives?

When I was beginning to develop the background for the Higbee clan, the family that is featured in *Anarchy at Almacks*, I thought of Arranmore. I loved the idea of a titled family that lived a modest life despite being tremendously wealthy. If I were the leader of that family, I would want everyone on the island to be happy. How would I accomplish that? Thus, the Isle of Edanmore in the Celtic Sea was born.

I still follow Arranmore on Facebook and have a copy of their calendar on my wall. It may not be a utopia, but that's how I envision it. One of these days, I hope that my husband and I will be able to visit there.

## The Regency Period

Writing about the Regency era is tricky. First there's the issue of which Regency era you're writing about — the actual historical regency era — 1811-1820 — or the years that led up to the historical regency era and then continued until Queen Victoria's marriage. (See the Glossary at the end of this book for a more information.)

Another issue is how to deal with the time period you are writing about and what is historically correct. As a reader, I like to know when things are happening. If the first chapter is preceded by the statement, "London, April, 1804," I'm very happy.

When a writer is that specific, it is appropriate to expect that the writer will know there can't be a scene where a waltz is danced at Almacks. The waltz wasn't introduced at Almacks until 1815, although it was danced on the European continent much earlier than that. That being said, if the exact date of a story is not specified, then a waltz at Almacks could be just fine.

## Accuracy in Punctuation and Spelling

Another issue has to do with punctuation and spelling. "Almacks" is a perfect example. In every Regency Romance I've ever read, the word Almacks is spelled Almack's. In an early draft of this novel, I spelled that word the same way. Then I came across the photograph of an actual voucher. It's the first image in this book. (See page 2.) As you can see, there is no apostrophe. It seemed to me that it would be more historically correct to present the name as it appeared on an actual voucher. Thus, Almacks without an apostrophe made its way into this novel and into the style sheet that I use to keep my writing consistent.

## Thank You, Dear Reader ...

... for reading Rowan's story. I hope that you enjoyed it. It was a wonderful adventure writing and bringing *Anarchy at Almacks* to life. More tales of the Flame Sisters are coming soon. Please visit *The Regency World of Nola Saint James* — nolasaintjames.com — for news of upcoming titles, blogs about the Regency World, 21st-Century Regency-themed experiences, merchandise, fun and games.

Wishing you success in all the endeavors that give you joy,

*Nola Saint James*

*Thank you.*

# ACKNOWLEDGMENTS

If it wasn't for the gracious, open-handed generosity
of Susan Rosenthal, Esq., this book might never have been
written. I had written *The Curse of the Ravenscrofft Brides*
some years ago and had been unable to get it published. I put
it on a shelf and gave up on the idea of a career as a novelist.

One wonderful weekend at Susan's Cottage by the Sea,
a very magical place on Long Island's North Fork, I found
myself making a confession to a long-time friend who was
also staying there. I told my friend, the gifted writer, artist
and publisher James W. Gaynor, a former editor at Grosset
and Dunlap, that I had a secret identity as a writer of Regency
Romances. I confessed that I had written a novel and asked if
he would take a look at it and tell me if it was any good. He
agreed to read it and tell me what he thought.

James's response, about a week later, was all that any
aspiring writer could hope for. He loved it and thought it was
publishable. That was the beginning of what has become a
dream creative collaboration.

Thank you, Susan, for your support, hospitality and
friendship all these years. Where you dwell, magic happens.
My gratitude has no bounds.

Jim, I give thanks every day to the Force in the Universe
that brought us together. You make me a better writer with
every conversation we have. You have opened up my world
in ways I would never have imagined. Your experience and
understanding of the world of business has made the Regency
World of Nola Saint James the special place that it is. I cherish
each moment we spend together. Thank you for being you.

Every word that a writer commits to the printed page is a reflection of that person's inner life. Exposing oneself is not always easy or comfortable. It is with deep gratitude that I acknowledge the help and support over the years of my brilliant therapist, Anita Gilodo. Without her support, love and encouragement, none of my stories would have seen the light of day. Thank you so much, Anita.

The crafting of Nola and her world has been a long process that has involved and continues to involve many people.

Heart-felt thanks to master calligrapher and artist Neil Howard Yerman for his creation of Nola's signature logo. He created a gem under difficult circumstances. Thank you so much.

Special thanks to Kelly Duke McKinley, our award-winning designer at The Shop Keys for the beautiful design of this book. You have set my words to music and I am immensely grateful.

Thank you also to Kelly's partner, Peter McKinley, our gifted website creator and the wonderful staff at The Shop Keys. Your artistry and attention to detail brought The Regency World of Nola Saint James to life and continues to enrich the Regency world esthetic and experience.

Madeline McKinley, thank you for your lovely illustrations. You brought this story to life on a very tight deadline. It is a pleasure to work with such a talented artist at the beginning of her professional career.

Thank you also to my long-time website collaborator, the estimable Jim Van Abbema, who assisted in trouble-shooting many technical details. You are, as you have always been, a rock.

Kudos to Josh Libatique at Pathbrand.com for outstanding SEO support and web services. I finally understand what the SEO process is all about. Thank you!

Public relations is a critical part of launching and growing any successful effort. Marla White, public relations, marketing and branding professional, whitehanded.com, has been and continues to be a dream partner. The sun shined brightly when we met. Thank you for focusing our mission so successfully and supporting it so brilliantly.

The proper management of social media is critical in communicating effectively with a wide audience. Thank you Rabbi David Paskin, The Torah Tech Guy, for introducing me to Brightseed Creative's CEO, Danielle Snyder. Danielle, you helped us navigate the shoals of digital marketing, social media management and content creation to develop a highly effective, results-oriented digital marketing strategy. With creativity, laser-sharp focus and gentle humor, you and your team helped the Regency World marketing group create a stunning and highly effective social media marketing campaign. Thank you so much! We look forward to many more successful collaborations.

Dealing with the world of distribution and Amazon marketing is a tremendous challenge. Ryan Child, you kept us sane and helped guide us through this really puzzling maze. Thank you so much for your excellent work and wise guidance.

Bringing Nola Saint James to life took the efforts of many people. I would especially like to thank our stylist, Jasmine Moya, for her skill, insight and good humor.

When an author finishes writing a book, having people one trusts read the first draft is a great gift. I would like to give special thanks to my very first Beta Reader, Marleen Schussler. Marleen, you loved the Ravenscrofft world and kept asking for more stories. Your enthusiasm helped me continue writing. Thank you so much for your support.

When I was five years old, my father, who was my first proofreader, taught me that a manuscript had to be perfect — free of any errors — before it could be submitted. I promised to commit myself to that goal. Little did I know that producing a manuscript without errors of any kind is a task of gargantuan proportions. I suspect that it may not be possible. All one can do is try. Many thanks must go to our Beta Reader/Proof Reader extraordinaire Jenny Rodriguez. What an amazing job you did in finding the many little niggly things that both James and I missed — although we read the manuscript at least 54 times. My father, the stickler, would be very proud of the work you did on this book.

Early on in the development of *The Regency World of Nola Saint James,* I knew that I wanted to include Regency era recipes in my books and on our website. Preparing and eating food of a Regency era and culture gives us a visceral understanding of peoples' lives.

I chose to present tea sandwiches in this particular book because it is a type of food that anyone can prepare. To make sure that my instructions were clear, I asked a number of friends to read my directions and to prepare one sandwich themselves and take a photo. My request met with a generous outpouring of support. The lovely photo taken by Zeita Lobley made it into the book. Thank you, Z for your enthusiastic support.

It is with deep appreciation that I acknowledge the thoughtful work of all the readers and copy editors, sandwich chefs and tea sandwich photographers. I am immensely grateful. Thanks go to: Trudy Brown, Ezra David, Lior David, Rabbi Laurie Gold, Sharon Kantowitz, Cathy Marx, Marlene Sklar, Marleen Schussler and Judith Wolf.

I am particularly blessed by the presence in my life of my Monday evening Bible as Literature cohort, The Bible Explorers. The support that I get from all of you gives me joy and energy to do the work that I do. Thank you, Alan, Emily, Jim, Marlene, Rebecca, Rona, Susan, Trudy and Zeita.

A writer may write in solitude, but it takes a family to sustain one through the ups and downs of the creative process as well as through life. I happily acknowledge the love and support that I constantly receive from my wonderful family: Justin and Judy, Lior and Ezra, Evan, Cathy, Andy, Ali, Chris and Ava.

Finally, to my dear spouse. Without you I would not have been able to complete this project. Your steadfastness, your love and your support through these many years mean everything to me. "From this day, hand in hand, as we have always been ... "

*Nola Saint James*

*How can Romance stories help us become our best selves?*

# BOOK CLUB DISCUSSION GUIDE

## What is Love at First Sight? Does it Really Exist?

It's 1804. Lord Maximillian Francis Browning, Viscount Darby, heir to the 7th Earl of Bainbridge, Max to his friends, is a handsome, desirable, titled and wealthy leader of London society. All the women want to catch his attention and all the men want to be him. He has an exciting secret career as a spy for the Admiralty. The last thing Max is thinking about is love.

Max and his best friend, Lord Richard Grey Birmingham, 9th Earl of Wellesly Glen, Grey to his friends, are attending a ball at Almacks, London's famous venue for bringing together unmarried young ladies and gentlemen. Invitation only! It's the first Wednesday of the Season and the room is buzzing with anticipation as a new crop of young ladies make their debuts in Society.

A stunning trio of red-haired young ladies have just entered the room. Everyone has turned to stare at them. One of the young women, a beauty with dark red hair seems to notice Max across the crowded room. Her expressive sapphire-blue eyes appear to see right through to the depths of his soul.

Max is stopped dead in his tracks. From somewhere deep within himself he hears a voice shout, "It is she!" And then, "Mine!" Thus begins the love story of Rowan Higbee and Max Browning. Before he can marry the woman, he has to meet her. As it turns out, that's not so easy!

Have you ever experienced the uncanny feeling of meeting someone and feeling immediately attracted to him or her? Do you know anyone who claims that meeting their partner was literally "love at first sight?" Is love at first sight a real thing? How does one know if it's really and truly love?

## How Do Early Experiences of Love Affect Adult Relationships?

Heroine Rowan Higbee has come to London to find a husband. For most of her life she has lived a mostly-charmed life with her parents, her two younger sisters and some of her eight half-brothers on Edanmore Island in the Celtic Sea. Her parents, Baron and Baroness Edanmore, rule their little world with love and kindness.

Everything is fine until a snake in the form of a handsome young stranger invades their Garden of Eden. Rowan believes that she loves him and he loves her. Her dreams are shattered when she discovers he is betrothed to another. Since then, Rowan has doubted her ability to love. She believes that no man will ever want her because she permitted her first love to take liberties with her person.

Now, several years later, she is drawn to a compelling stranger across a crowded ballroom. Rowan feels an undeniable attraction to him. She worries that if he were to learn her secret, he would reject her. What's a girl to do?

How do early experiences of attraction, sexual awakening and love affect one's understanding of oneself? How do these perceptions affect the choices that one makes? What are ways in which one can disconnect from negative self-judgement in order to enter into healthy adult relationships? How can romance stories help us to become our best selves?

## What Can Women Do to Empower Themselves to Achieve Their Goals?

Rowan has two sisters with whom she is very close. While each sister has her own special interests and skills, they often work together to achieve their goals. They are also lucky enough to be surrounded by adults who believe that young women should be supported in achieving their dreams. When someone fires a gun at the sisters while they are riding their horses in Hyde Park, the three sisters immediately turn and race toward the stand of trees where they believe that the shots came from.

Their brother, Benedict, and Max and Grey are horrified. Max tries to rescue Rowan, thinking that her horse has run away with her. She attacks him with her fists for his trouble!

In the "real world," women face many obstacles when they attempt to live their best lives and realize their dreams. The ability of a woman to become self-empowered requires developing allies with similar objectives and similar points of view. How might one do this? Is it possible for a man to be a real ally? Can other women be allies? Discuss the ways in which women, and possibly men, can work together so that women can lead their best lives.

*Bedlam in Bath*

WILLOW'S STORY

*Nola Saint James*

THE EDANMORE CHRONICLES
BOOK TWO

**And now a peek at**

*Bedlam in Bath*

**COMING SOON!**

**A stately Georgian home**
**in the Royal Crescent, Bath May, 1804**

It was not a dark and stormy night. The three women gathered in a circle were not ragged, wart-nosed hags. The brew before them did not contain eye of newt or toe of frog. It was midday. The sun was shining. A soft spring breeze was playing with the new growth of leaves in the trees of Sydney Gardens. The three women were all of a certain age, their garments and coiffures announcing to all the world their elevated social status.

They sat around a delicate rosewood table, a beautiful Wedgewood blue jasperware tea set before them. The brew gently steeping in the covered pot was Lapsang Souchong. And yet, a male fly on the wall would not be wrong in coming to the conclusion that these three were up to no good. At least as far as the bachelor status of a particular gentleman was concerned.

Lady Honoria Elsbeth Prelling, Lady Barbara Marie Prelling and Lady Caroline Heath Prelling Stainbridge, Dowager Viscountess Dilling, were the maternal aunts of one Lord Richard Grey Birmingham, 9th Earl of Wellesly Glen. Grey to his friends.

Grey loved these aunts, his mother's older sisters, and they loved him. He was the son that none of them had ever been blessed to bring into the world. These women had been scrupulous in seeing to it, throughout Grey's years away at school, that he always had a hamper full of treats from Fortnum & Mason to stave off hunger at odd hours of the day

*"How fortunate that we didn't let our house next door this season."*

or night. Even when he was at Cambridge, they made sure that he received a regular delivery.

For the last few years, as Grey's 30th birthday approached, he had kept his distance from Bath, their home. His aunts were matchmaking for him. He knew it as surely as he knew every inch of his cozy London apartment where he lived in low key, bachelor splendor. Grey valued his single state too much to fall into his aunts' snares. There was plenty of time for him to marry.

He was correct, of course, about their plans. Had he been that fly on the wall on that lovely spring day, he would have fled to the continent on the very next ship. Grey's aunts were hatching a plan.

The aunts had finally had enough of their nephew's evasions. They had just received a startling letter from their sister Heloise, Grey's mother. She informed them that Grey's best friend, Lord Maximillian Francis Browning had just married the eldest daughter of the fabulously wealthy Baron Edanmore. The letter had definitely set a fox amongst the chickens.

"Grey stood up for Max at the church," read Lady Caroline, the official reader of letters. She was the youngest of the three sisters and possessed the best vision.

"Heloise said that Grey walked into St George's as cool as you please and didn't twitch a muscle." Looking up and gazing at her sisters she said, "That the roof of that venerable church didn't fall in is a sign!"

"Indeed," exclaimed Lady Honoria, the eldest sister. "The good Lord is telling us that it is time to ACT!"

"We must strike while the iron is hot, sisters! There is no time to lose!" exclaimed Lady Barbara Marie, the middle sister and the most volatile. Lady Barbara always spoke in exclamation points.

"Max will be on his wedding trip and Grey will be all alone! He must come here and bear us company! We will alleviate his loneliness over the loss of his good friend!" continued Lady Barbara Marie. "We can help him mourn his friend's loss of his bachelor status."

Sister Honoria giggled.

"An excellent idea," she said. "But if he comes alone, he won't have anyone young to keep him company. Perhaps Max's wife's sisters would accompany him. My correspondents tell me that the three girls are very close. Surely they will be missing their eldest sister."

"There is an unmarried brother as well, presently escorting his sisters around London. He should be invited too," suggested Lady Caroline. "And the baron and baroness, of course."

"Of course," chimed in Lady Honoria. "I understand that they are a very lovely couple. We must distract them from the sadness of parting with their eldest daughter!"

"They must all stay with us," said Lady Caroline. "How fortunate that we didn't rent our house next door this season. We can open up the adjoining wing and we'll all be one happy family!"

"Fortunate indeed," said Lady Barbara. "That clear-eyed gypsy woman from Symonds Yat who told our fortunes last All Hallows' Eve at the Winston's Ball told you to keep the house empty this Season. You listened to her advice! At the time, I wondered about your credulity. As always, your instincts were right!"

"We're going to have a grand time!" laughed Lady Honoria.

"Grey won't get away this time!" Lady Caroline chortled. "By this time next year, we may very well be great aunties!"

"Ooooh! Babies! I love babies!" crooned Lady Barbara.

The three sisters looked at one another and sighed with happiness. They all loved plans! And their plans were always successful! Why should this situation be any different? Their nephew Grey was only a man, after all!

*She was handed a cup of tea and a plate with several tea sandwiches and a slice of cake.*

# Tea Sandwiches, Anyone?*

What is the difference between a sandwich and a tea sandwich, you may ask? In Regency terms, a sandwich is by definition two slices of bread with a filling. Unless the term "sandwich" is qualified, a sandwich is a substantial meal or snack. The bread is thickly sliced, slathered with something, generally mustard or butter and filled with one or more ample portions of meat and or cheese. Men eat sandwiches of this type.

A tea sandwich is a completely different comestible. In Regency times, among the aristocracy, small-waisted women were highly prized. In London, during the Season, even a very thin woman would be careful not to let a man see her eat any normal amount of food, thinking that it would put him off. He might think that she had an appetite for physical things — like food — and fear that with time, she might grow fat.

At ton balls, Venetian breakfasts and other parties, women who were concerned about their figures, ate little or nothing. A young, unmarried woman who was looking for a husband in London, if she was less than sylph-thin, would not eat any food in the presence of a man in public. Even at a dinner party in her own home, she would be very careful about what she ate. No woman would ever eat the type of sandwich described above in public if she hoped to find a suitable husband.

On the other hand, aristocratic women spent much of their daytime hours in London visiting one another. It was considered polite to offer one's guest tea and some sort of food — small pastries, slices of cake and biscuits. (English biscuits are what Americans call cookies.) If the gathering was later in the day, it was considered appropriate to offer something more substantial. However, even when women were alone, they made judgements about what one another ate and one another's figures. At some point — no one knows exactly when — some inventive hostess had her cook create a female version of the sandwich — the tea sandwich.

A tea sandwich is, by definition, small and thin. It is a finger food that can be eaten in 2-3 bites at most. It is dainty. The crusts are cut off the bread. The sandwich is cut either in a thin rectangle or in a triangular shape. It has the minimum amount of filling possible. A tea sandwich consists of one section of what today would be considered a whole sandwich.

When a woman eats a tea sandwich, she looks delicate, almost as though she is barely eating at all. No one would dare to suggest that a lady who chooses to eat a tea sandwich is a glutton. Best of all, because of the sandwich's delicacy, a lady may even eat a tea sandwich in the company of an eligible man without causing him to think of her as stuffing her mouth or filling her stomach.

In the gastronomy of Regency England, tea sandwiches are the easiest item to prepare while giving the hostess a wide range of options. There are a few simple rules, easily mastered, for making tea sandwiches and inventing fillings.

# Jane Austen Alert!

Jane Austen is the patron saint of Regency romance writers and readers. She had a lot to say about food in the Regency era. Therefore, I feel compelled to add a comment about Austen, food and young women eating in public.

*Portrait of Jane Austen circa 1873*

In Jane's stories, people were always having dinners, parties with a great deal of food and lavish picnics. The women in Austen's stories did not seem to worry about eating food in front of men. This being said, Jane primarily wrote about the gentry rather than the aristocracy. Most of her stories were set in the country rather than in London.

During the beginning of the 19th century, there was a big difference in manners and mores between the gentry and the aristocracy, between life in the country and life in London. Women in London and women in the country seem to have had different ideas and customs about how, where and what was acceptable with respect to dining, especially when men were present.

*Photo by Zeita Lobley*

## WWLE?
## What Would Ladies Eat?

**Basic Rules for Assembling a Tea Sandwich.**
(Sometimes called a Finger Sandwich)

1. Use fresh, thinly sliced bread. This is where commercially-sliced bread actually shines. Some manufacturers brand their bread as Thin Sliced or Very Thin. This type of bread is ideal for making this type of sandwich. Artisanal bread can be used, but it must be professionally sliced. A slice of about ¼" thick generally works best. If the bread seems too thick, flatten it with a rolling pin.

2. **Do not toast the bread!** Tea sandwiches are supposed to be soft and light as air.

3. Cut off all the crusts. Always. This makes the sandwiches look "sophisticated."

4. If making more than one sandwich, follow these steps.
   - Set up the slices in two rows on your work area.
   - One row is the bread that will get the flavoring agent — butter, mustard, mayonnaise.
   - The facing row is the bread that will get the filling.

5. Always put a very thin layer of flavoring on one slice of bread. This could be butter, soft cheese, mustard,

mayonnaise or good quality olive oil. For sandwiches with sweet or sweet and savory fillings, one might use jam, preserves or honey. Some recipes call for flavoring on both sides of the bread. This is very much the chef's choice.

6. The filling can either go between two pieces of flavored bread or on a slice that has not been flavored.

7. The filing can be restricted to one ingredient — a single slice of cheese — for example, or it can have a second complementary component such as a wafer-thin slice of cucumber or a small lettuce leaf.

8. If using a filling like tuna or egg salad, only use enough so that the bread has the lightest possible coating. Keep all fillings away from the borders of the slice.

9. When all the slices of bread have been prepared, match them up and cut them.

10. A tea sandwich is cut in half, either length-wise, to create a rectangle, or diagonally, to make a triangle.

11. If not serving immediately, cover the sandwiches with a lightly dampened cloth, paper towel or plastic wrap. Refrigerate, but take them out a few minutes prior to serving so that the sandwiches are not cold. Keep them covered until serving.

**Remember:** The idea is for the sandwich to look like the merest "nothing." It should taste fabulous.

## Tea Sandwich Fillings

Some fillings are iconic, like the cucumber sandwich. Both slices of bread are buttered, and several wafer-thin cucumbers nestle between the two slices. Here are some other options.

**Note for Vegans:** There are many vegan butters, cheeses and other types of spreads that can be used for vegan tea sandwiches. Enjoy!

## The Classic Cucumber Sandwich

Peel the cucumbers and cut them as thin as possible. Salt the sliced cucumbers and put them aside. Prepare the bread with butter on both pieces of bread. Pour off any liquid that has resulted from salting the cucumbers. Dry them with a towel. Create a layer of cucumbers on one of the pieces of bread. If the cucumbers are really thin, two layers is fine. Cover the cucumbers with the other slice of bread. Cut and serve.

## Variations:

While not traditional, there are many ways to customize this classic. Instead of butter, use hummus or a soft, spreadable cheese, add a layer of thinly sliced radish, add freshly ground pepper, incorporate some chopped herbs into the butter or even a drop of truffle oil. Top with a sprig of arugula or fresh chives.

### Vegan Twist

Instead of butter, substitute Fortnum & Mason's Vegan Chilli and Paprika Mayonnaise.**

## Truffle Delight

*Featuring Fortnum & Mason Minced Black Truffle or Truffle Oil*

Add a small amount of Fortnum & Mason minced black truffle or truffle oil to sweet butter and use it to flavor bread for a sliced egg sandwich. A variation is to flavor the bread with mayonnaise and flavor the egg salad with one of these products.

## Sliced Egg or Egg Salad
**(or any other type of "salad" filling)**
Flavor the bread with either plain or flavored mayonnaise, top with very finely chopped egg salad or thin hard-boiled egg slices. Gently season the eggs with salt, if desired, freshly-ground pepper, a dash of curry powder or paprika.

## Smoked Salmon
Flavor both pieces of bread with a thin layer of any spreadable mild cheese. Cover one slice of bread with a very thinly-sliced piece of smoked salmon. If desired, top with a little chopped dill, a few capers or a splash of lemon juice.

## Chutney and Cheese
Mix a small amount (to taste) of any fruit chutney (i.e. Major Grey's Mango) into softened cream cheese. Spread a thin layer on both pieces of bread. Top with a thin slice of fruit — either fresh or preserved. For example, if using mango chutney, top with a thin slice of very ripe mango. **To make an easy chutney,** use either apricot, peach or pineapple jam. Mix with curry powder to taste. One can also add a little garlic powder if desired. Add a little water or sherry to get the right consistency.

## The Mediterranean
Apply a thin layer of hummus (any savory flavor) to both sides of the bread. Cover one slice with a mixture of thin pickle and grated carrots. Other options include sliced egg with a little harissa (hot sauce) and toasted pine nuts and grated carrots.

## The American

Apply a thin layer of any type of nut butter — peanut, almond, cashew — smooth or crunchy, on one slice of bread and the jelly or jam of your choice on the other slice. Enjoy! If you like, add a layer of thinly sliced bananas and/or mini marshmallows.

## Meat and/or Cheese

Flavor one slice with mustard, mayonnaise or butter. On the other slice put 1 thin slice of the meat of your choice and one thin slice of cheese. Or double up on the meat or go cheese only.

## Fruit and Cheese

Apply a thin coat of your favorite spreadable cheese on both pieces of the bread. Cover one piece with the thinly sliced fresh fruit of your choice — apple, pear, strawberry, mango. For more variety, use two different flavors of cheese, one on each slice of bread.

## Fruit and Cheese – British Style

A variation of the Fruit and Cheese sandwich is to use a good-quality jam or marmalade instead of the fruit. For an authentic English take on this sandwich, use a good quality English cheese and pair it with Fortnum & Mason's Old English Hunt Marmalade.

## Walnut Raisin

Use walnut raisin bread for this sandwich. Spread each slice with cream cheese. If desired, cover the cheese with chopped walnuts or other nuts and a few raisins.

## Sliced Avocado or Smashed Avocado

**Sliced** — Spread a little Russian dressing on each side of the bread. Put a piece if lettuce or arugula on each slice. Cover one piece of bread with thinly-sliced ripe avocado. Season with freshly-ground pepper, a splash of lemon juice and some capers if desired.

**Smashed** — Spread a little thick salsa on one slice of bread. Spread guacamole on the other slice. If desired, sprinkle with some freshly-chopped cilantro.

## Enjoy!

** Fortnum & Mason ships non-perishable items to the United States and many other countries. Williams Sonoma carries a line of Fortnum & Mason products in the United States.

*Rregency Romance Words and Phrases*

Many years ago, I read a story set in Regency England in which a group of men were making a bet on something. One man bet a pony. I remember wondering why someone would bet an equine when everyone else was betting money? It was some time before I learned that the word *pony* was Regency slang for 25 pounds sterling!

One of the joys of reading historical fiction is encountering new words and concepts. This is particularly true of Regency England, which had a very rich vocabulary. With the exception of the discussion of the terms Regency and Cockney, all the words in this glossary can be found in *Anarchy at Almacks*. These terms refer to manners, customs and mores in Great Britain during the literary Regency era.

For an introduction to the whys and wherefores of historical fiction and its details, see my blog *Historical Fiction: Why It's So Compelling* at nolasaintjames.com

## Regency – A General Introduction

If you search the internet for the definition of the Regency era, you may quickly become very confused. There are many different ideas presented about when the Regency era in England actually took place. The following is offered as a general guide.

For *literary* purposes, the Regency Fiction Writers define the Regency era in Great Britain as 1780-1840. This covers the years during which King George III's mental and physical health was declining and his eldest son, George, the Prince of Wales, was beginning to be positioned to take his father's place. It also includes the ascension to the throne of the Prince of Wales as George IV – 1820, and his younger brother William's succession after George IV's death in 1830 as King William IV.

King William IV died in 1837. He was succeeded by Princess Victoria, the eldest surviving grandchild of King George III. She was 18 at the time that she became Queen. In 1840, she married Prince Albert. The end of the literary Regency era roughly coincides with the marriage of Queen Victoria.

For *historical* purposes, the Regency era began in 1811. King George's health had deteriorated to the point where he could no longer rule. The Prince of Wales (era referred to as Prinny) was formally named Prince Regent so that he could officially act for the King. The historical Regency era only lasted from 1811 – 1820. When King George III died in 1820, Prinny became King and took the name George IV. This was the technical end of the historical Regency era.

## Cockney – (page 90)

Cockney is an English dialect primarily spoken by working-class Londoners living in the East End of London.

In literature, it is often used to signify a character who is poor and/or uneducated. Cockney has its own vocabulary and makes liberal use of rhymes. For example, one's *trouble and strife* is one's wife.

## Dowager – (page 19)

The term dowager pertains to a titled woman who is widowed. For example, the wife of the Earl of Devon would be known as the Countess of Devon as long as the Earl was alive. If the earl pre-deceased her, she would become known as the Dowager Countess of Devon. A man's title did not change if his wife predeceased him. An earl was always an earl unless he was given a more elevated title.

## Fortnum & Mason – (page 235)

Fortnum & Mason is an upscale specialty foods department store in London, England. The main store is located at 181 Piccadilly in the St James's area of London. It was established there in 1707 by William Fortnum and Hugh Mason. Today, there are additional stores in London and at Heathrow Airport. Fortnum's also ships to many countries and their products are available at specialty food stores around the world. The store is famous for its food hampers. (Americans, think "gift baskets.") Fans of the television series, All Things Great and Small, will recognize the food hampers sent to Uncle Herriott by Tricki Woo as coming from Fortnum's.

## Horse Terms

**Cattle** – (page 85)

Regency slang for horses

**Gelding** – (page 101)

A male horse that has been castrated (had his testicles removed.) Male horses that are not intended for breeding are gelded to inhibit aggressive tendencies. This makes them more amenable to training as riding horses and working animals.

**Hack** – (page 107)

A horse with a good disposition and calm manner. A hack would be particularly suitable for an inexperienced or recreational rider.

**To hack out, go on a hack** – Generally a recreational ride outside of an arena.

## Maze – (page 141)

A maze is a three-dimensional puzzle. One enters the maze and attempts to navigate a series of paths in order to make one's way to the center. The term maze is based on a Middle English word that translates as 'delirium' or 'delusion'. In the sixteenth century, hedge mazes (mazes created by planting and trimming bushes suitable for this endeavor) were created by European royalty as entertainment for guests. Mazes also provided private places for lovers to meet. The United Kingdom's oldest surviving hedge maze is found at Hampton Court. It was commissioned around 1700 by William III.

## Modiste – (page 20)

A woman who designed and produced fashionable attire for women. Also, one who would provide advice on fashion and fashion trends. In Regency England, French modistes were preferred. Some English fashion designers affected a French accent in order to be more desirable to their aristocratic clients.

## Mort – (page 90)

Cockney slang for the word woman.

## Stillroom – (page 97)

The stillroom was a place, often off the kitchen, where medicines, cosmetics, cleaning products, soap, essential oils and flavorings were prepared. Beer and wine might also be prepared in a still room. Until these products became commercially available at reasonable prices in the mid-to-late 19th century, most homes maintained some sort of stillroom. The lady of the house was usually in charge of the stillroom and she passed her secrets on to her daughters.

## To Call Someone Out – (page 122)

To challenge someone to a duel, almost always over a matter of honor. Only men of the aristocracy dueled with one another. An aristocrat would not challenge a man of a lower class to a duel nor would he accept a challenge from a man who was not an aristocrat. Dueling was technically illegal but prosecutions related to duels were extremely rare. There were a great many rules about duels and how they were to be conducted.

# *Want to Read More About the Regency Era?*

**I really enjoyed these books. I think you will too.**

***The Time Traveler's Guide to Regency Britain: A Handbook for Visitors to 1789 — 1830,*** Ian Mortimer, Pegasus Books, New York, London.

This is a wonderful look at the broader Regency era in Great Britain – 1789 – 1830. In 12 well-written essays, Mortimer paints a vivid picture of the people and events  of this extremely important time in Great Britain's history. Quite a few lovely illustrations with enlightening captions. Excellent endnotes and a very detailed index.

***The Regency Revolution, Jane Austen, Napoleon, Lord Byron and the Making of the Modern World.*** Robert Morrison, Atlantic Books, London

Almost everything one would like to know about the historical Regency period — 1811 – 1820. The story is told in short, pithy essays that are well-written and extremely readable. A wide variety of illustrations help to illuminate the text. This reads like a novel, but is quite scholarly. Substantial  number of endnotes and a very good index. Readers who are interested in the actual Regency period will find this book to be an excellent resource.

***What Jane Austen Ate and Charles Dickens Knew: From Fox Hunting to Whist – the Facts of Daily Life in 19th-Century England,*** Daniel Pool, Simon and Schuster, 1993

Although published in 1993, this book stands the test of time. It covers the entire 19th-Century rather than just the Regency Period. If you want to find out "How to Address Your Betters," or when Michaelmas Term started, this is the book for you. Features an extensive glossary, an excellent bibliography and a very good index. You have almost anything  you would want to know about this time period in one concise volume. Although out of print, it is easy to find a copy online and the cost of a volume is very reasonable. A fun read.

***Jane Austen's Pride and Prejudice: The Classic Novel with Recipes for Modern Teatime Treats.***
Martha Stewart, Puffin Plated, New York

This is Jane Austen's Pride and Prejudice, but with a charming twist. The text is illustrated throughout with magnificently decorated cookies! 12 Martha Stewart recipes for  baked goods are featured and will surely make one's next tea party a real hit. The recipes are well-written and easy to follow. A perfect gift for an Austen fan and/or your favorite baker.

***Jane Austen's Wardrobe,*** Hilary Davidson, Yale University Press, New Haven and London, 2023

Renowned fashion historian, Hilary Davidson, has produced a swoon-worthy new book based on Austen's 161 known letters, as well as her own surviving garments and accessories. In this deep dive into Jane Austen's closet, a new portrait of the iconic Regency writer appears. Beautifully designed and packed with photographs and illustrations. Excerpts from Austen's letters and Davidson's probing questions make reading this book a truly remarkable experience.

To prepare for reading Jane Austen's Wardrobe, one might wish to acquire an earlier book by the same author, *Dress in the Age of Jane Austen: Regency Fashion.* This book is also rich in full- color illustrations. It presents an extremely  learned and broad view of the intersection of fashion and society in the Regency period. A wonderful resource for anyone interested in the Regency era.